Nicodemus

The night visitor

Keith Ballard Farris

iUniverse, Inc.
New York   Bloomington

Nicodemus

The night visitor

iUniverse books may be ordered through booksellers or by contacting:

iUniverse
1663 Liberty Drive
Bloomington, IN 47403
www.iuniverse.com
1-800-Authors (1-800-288-4677)

ISBN: 978-1-4502-5979-8 (sc)
ISBN: 978-1-4502-5980-4 (ebook)

Printed in the United States of America

iUniverse rev. date: 09/21/2010

Introduction to Nicodemus

Many have taken upon themselves to write the story of Jesus of Nazareth. Of those I have read, I seldom encounter the Jesus I know from the Bible record. I have taken the encounters recorded in John's gospel where the lives of Nicodemus and Jesus intersect to write a fictional, yet hopefully plausible, narrative.

The very fact that the apostle John chooses to mention Nicodemus three times in his gospel, written near the end of the first century, is probably highly significant. The details are lost in the dust of history.

Keith Ballard Farris

Acknowledgments

I am deeply indebted to three people who helped in this effort: My son, Brian, for his patient corrections and careful reading; my daughter, Leigh, for her strong encouragements and gentle suggestions; and finally, my wife, Lyn, for many hours of careful proof reading. Without these three, I would not have completed this work. Thanks to Patty Slack for her editing expertise. I also thank Nate Lollar for reading and suggesting changes to the manuscript. For the front piece, I thank Lois Douglass for her very artistic and appropriate sketch.

Sources:

Some scripture quotations taken from The New American Standard Bible® (1977 edition). Copyright © 1977 by The Lockman Foundation. Used by permission. (www.Lockman.org)

Some scriptures taken from the Holy Bible, New International Version®, NIV®. Copyright© 1973, 1978, 1984 by Biblica, Inc.™. Used by permission of Zondervan. All rights reserved worldwide. (www.zondervan.com)

Mazar, Maier. Josephus, The Jewish War. Cornfeld, ed. Grand Rapids, Mich.: Zondervan, 1982.

The New International Standard Bible Encyclopaedia James Orr, general Editor
Hendrickson Pub. 1939, 1956 Wm. B. Eerdmans, Pub, third printing

Chapter One

JUDEA, 5 BC

Nicky felt the warmth and inhaled the fragrance of the fresh bread he pressed to his chest. Suddenly, he felt his sister's hand clutch his arm.

"Quick, get in here!" She jerked him into the opening between two buildings.

He saw two Roman soldiers appear in the street ahead. In the shadows of evening, it was hard to tell if they had seen Nicky or his older sister.

Joanna whispered, "Don't make a sound."

Sure enough, Nicky heard the clomp of the caligae—Roman boots with hob-nails—on the hard-packed street. His heart thudded, but he knew his sister would be the one they were interested in. Only last month, another young girl had been forced to spend a night with the soldiers, and her life changed forever. He wondered if this messiah who was supposed to be coming would change anything. The rabbis spoke of a new king, but right now Romans were in charge.

In the shadowy light, the two watched the shapes pause at the opening between the houses. They pressed their backs against the cold plaster, hardly breathing. Time seemed to stop. Then the soldiers shuffled off down the narrow street.

When it was quiet, Nicky and Joanna crept to the street, glancing both ways. They scrambled toward home. Several times they ducked into doorways. Nicky's mouth felt dry. Once they reached their own street, he could hear the welcome laughter from the house. They dashed to the doorway. Nicky banged the door behind them, panting. Nicky saw the tears running down Joanna's cheeks.

Their mother, Muriel, turned Joanna toward her. "A problem?"

Joanna gulped. "Two soldiers, but we hid."

Muriel's brow wrinkled. "I knew we should have sent the men for the bread." She drew Joanna close. "I'm sorry, darling ... I'm so sorry." She took the bread—now squashed in the middle—from Nicky and, with the other hand, tousled his curly hair. "Neither of you should have been out after dark."

Nicky dropped beside his cousin Joseph, who sat on the floor listening to the three older men. Joanna picked up little Jessie and rocked him. The other women were working in the cooking area, preparing food for the next day. Nicky stared at the three men and wondered how three brothers could be so different. His father, Barak, was wide with a simple robe and only a circle of hair. Cousin Joseph's father, Joram, was tall, his head covered with gray hair and his chin with a beard reaching his shoulders. The youngest brother, Zedekiah, probably weighed as much as the other two together. His silky, blue robe barely covered his portly figure. His gold rings matched his robe's decorations.

Barak's fists clenched. "The only reason for this census is so the Romans can tax away our whole nation. And to think my brother would become a publican servant of Quirinius."

Joram leaned forward. "I have not become a publican. Just because Herod enlisted those of us who are scribes to help with this enrollment, it does not mean we have become tax collectors. When this task is done, I will return to Arimathea and grow my olives and dates."

Zedekiah chuckled. "I can't get over it; an avowed Pharisee is collecting taxes." His large belly pulsed. "I suppose it would have been worse if you were a Zealot."

Barak slapped his hand on his leg. "I don't want us to argue politics tonight. Tomorrow this cursed census begins." He turned toward Joram. "What time do you meet to begin the work?"

"At the third hour we meet in the market place where our tasks will be assigned and parchments handed out. I hear the enrollment will begin later in the day, or on the morrow."

Zedekiah snickered. "It's still hard to imagine this many descendents of Jessie in this small a town. Between David's and Solomon's offspring, this village is probably more crowded than any town in Judea. Even Jerusalem and Hebron have more room." He turned to his brother. "Barak, you are a scholar of the writings. Did anyone ever figure out how many wives and kids old Solomon had, anyway? I hear he had more wives and concubines than there were days in a year."

Muriel's voice cut the air. "We will not talk about that." She glared at her brother-in-law, then turned to her daughter. "You need to put Jessie to bed in the boys' room. We will move his basket later. It is also time for Nicodemus to be in bed. One week from tomorrow he will be standing in the temple, before all, to read the Torah. He must study hard this week."

Nicky was frustrated. He pleaded, "But, Mother, I know my Torah passages ... I know them well. Couldn't I stay up with Joseph?"

"Joseph may stay up if his father allows, but remember, he is two years older and he has already done his rite of passage." She turned to the men. "Joram, you and your family will take the children's bedroom, and, Zedekiah, you and your wife will use our bedroom. Barak, the baby, and I will sleep here." She faced her son. "Joanna will help me finish here and then she will join you on the roof. Now get your bedding and run along."

Nicky clutched the blankets under his arm and started up the worn outside stairs to the rooftop. It was a balmy night. He listened to his relatives' laughter. Straw crunched under his sandals as he mounted the stairs. Two opposing ideas struggled in his mind. Why could his cousin and older sister get to stay and talk while he was sent to bed? Still, his own quiet space under the stars was comforting. He yawned; it'd been a long day. In the distance he could see the lights of Jerusalem. Though the moon was but a sliver, one star was brilliant, its light illuminating everything. He could see his mother's date palms in their big pots, and her red and blue robe hanging on the rope in the corner. He looked across the flat roofs. Most houses had lights and he knew many homes would be full of kinfolk. People from all over the nation of Israel were here. He wouldn't be the only one sleeping on a roof tonight.

He spread his blanket near the west side where he could get the first light of dawn. He stared at the bright star directly over-head. It lit everything. As Nicky lay gazing at the heavens, his eyelids drooped.

His mind revisited the events of the last week and the visit of the tall scholar from Jerusalem named Gamaliel. The teacher's eyes blazed as he told his stories, his arms moving wildly. His voice was sometimes soft, then thundering, as he re-told the ancient stories of their Jewish heritage. He held the class of thirteen-year-old boys spell-bound. Nicky shuddered recalling his description of the jagged Mount Sinai. He pulled his blanket close as he thought of the plague of snakes crawling among the terrified Israelites. He could almost hear their screams of terror—it sent goose bumps up his spine. The Torah had never seemed so real as when this scholar spoke. Nicky vividly remembered his description of the brazen serpent—Gamaliel called it Nekhushtan—the one Moses lifted high on a forked pole. Nicky imagined the twisting brass serpent and swarms of people fighting to gaze at it and feel its healing power.

He cuddled in his blanket and glanced around the roof to assure himself no snakes were on his house top. His eyes grew heavy.

The stars were still bright when Nicky bolted awake; his dreams of serpents caused his breath to come quickly. Then he heard it. To the south, a faint sound—someone singing, beautiful singing. He blinked, making sure he was awake. Tightening his robe, he stood and kicked into his sandals. He listened once more. The singing was still there. People downstairs were talking. He rushed down the stairs.

He burst in the door. "Father, someone's singing south of the city. There are lights on the hills."

Barak turned. "Son, it's late. You were sent to bed long ago." He shook his head. "Remember, next week you take your time of testing. You need your rest."

"But Father, someone is singing ... It's beautiful. Come." Nicky grabbed his father's arm.

Uncle Zedekiah crossed his hands behind his head. "My boy, many men consider themselves great singers when they celebrate with too much wine."

Nicky pretended to ignore his uncle. "Father, this is not drunken men; it is even more glorious than the singers of the temple. From our roof you can hear it clearly. And, Father, it is not coming from Herodium in the east, it's to the south and it's closer."

"Son, I know your visit to the temple is a memory you will not forget, but perhaps you dreamed ..." Barak stroked his cheek, looking at his wide-eyed son. He sighed, rose and walked to the door. "I'll come."

As Nicky led, the rest—one by one—followed. The stars were still as bright, and the one directly over them even more radiant. Nicky heard the music, but as he reached the landing, it died away. He turned to his father. He could tell he'd heard it, too.

His mother whispered, "Barak, it was singing, not his imagination."

The adults stood speechless in the glowing evening.. The sky was still. Finally, Barak broke the stillness. "It's stopped. Now it's time for all of us to rest. Perhaps tomorrow we'll learn the source of the music." He walked to the stairs. "Sleep well. Tomorrow the census begins."

On the quiet roof, Nicky had almost drifted off to sleep again when he heard shouts. Peeking over the edge, he heard a door bang open. His father strode into the street below. Several roughly-clad men were coming down the street, yelling.

Barak moved to the center of the street, blocking their way. "It's the middle of the night! Show some respect! People are asleep in this village." His commanding voice echoed through the street.

One of the strangers, carrying the long curved staff of a shepherd, grabbed Barak by both shoulders. "He's come—the Messiah has come!"

Uncle Joram, joining the crowd, stood beside his brother. "What did you just say?"

Another of the shepherds blurted, "Angels appeared. They say the Messiah is born ... We were to come and see this great thing!"

Uncle Zedekiah pushed forward. "In the middle of the night?" He guffawed. "The Messiah is born in the night, and a bunch of shepherds imagine a story by an angel? What have you men been drinking?"

The first shepherd faced Joram. "Where is the baby, the one born this night?"

The other shepherd moved down the street. "Come on, these men know nothing. Let's find someone who does. There is an innkeeper; he may have heard." The band of ragged men hurried down the street.

Uncle Zedekiah laughed. "These messianic Jews ... they even make the rabble believe them. Who ever heard of a king being born in a poor village like Bethlehem?"

Chapter Two

Rite of Passage

The sun peeked over the eastern hills. Nicky threw off his cover as a rooster crowed in the distance. The creak of the town's well cover being pushed aside by those needing to draw water announced a new day. The air was fresh. He stretched and looked at the few scattered clouds. He pulled his yarmulke from his cloak, put it on his head and turned toward the temple in Jerusalem. He lifted his hands and spoke softly. "Oh, Yahweh ..."

Just as he finished his morning psalm, he yawned again. He started to open the scroll beside him but hesitated. He could do it by memory. He lifted his head. *"Elleh haddebarim.* This is the commandment, the statutes and the judgments which the Lord your God has commanded me to teach you ..." He was unaware his voice had risen and someone was listening. He finished his long recitation with the *shema*: "Hear O Israel: The Lord is our God, the Lord is one."

Bowing, he felt a glow. He'd not forgotten a word. He was ready to become a son of the covenant.

"Your memory is good, my little brother. Your mind surpasses those of most of your classmates." The soft voice was Joanna's. "I hear the sounds of Mother's singing. She prepares our morning meal. Come. We will fetch water."

Nicky rolled his blankets and glanced at his sister. Her long black hair glistened in the sun. Her trim figure had filled out. She was almost a woman; this sixteenth year had brought many changes.

* * *

Nicky dropped his pail in the dirt. Three women were at the well before them.

The thin one chided, "I tell you, the rabbi said that this town of David would be the place where he is to be born."

The bent one snorted. "Our rabbi likes to invent stories about the prophecies. Those shepherds that awakened the whole village last night ... they have no concern for anyone's sleep. Messiah, hah!"

The third one sneered, tying her bucket to the rope. "Old woman, how many comings have been predicted in the last five years? There have been more messiah sightings than new buildings started by old King Herod himself."

Nicky wanted to mention the singing, but he knew the women wouldn't pay attention to a mere boy. He filled his pails in silence.

Heading homeward, pails sloshing, Nicky asked, "Joanna, did you hear the singing last night?"

Joanna's brown eyes were wide. "I was standing on the stairs. It was beautiful." They were silent as they walked on. Reaching the door she turned. "I've never heard singing like that ... never."

"Could the Messiah have come?" Nicky studied her face.

"I just don't know. But suppose ... just suppose ..." She turned and opened the door.

*   *   *

One week later, in the temple square, Nicky felt the stiffness of his new garment. He studied the intricate design on the cuff. His uncle Zedekiah was indeed generous—if only he were as prompt as he was rich. The group of fourteen men stood in a semi-circle around Nicky and his uncles. They were near enough to the stairs opening down to the Court of the Gentiles, so the women below could see and hear the men perform the ceremony. Nicky wished the law would allow women up into this inner court.

He watched his father glance toward the Beautiful Gate, then at the sun. It was past time for them to begin. Nicky knew special permission to use the inner courtyard had been granted to his father because of his position. As the sun rose high, more and more priests were hurrying about the huge inner court. To the east, worshipers brought sheep, goats and small birds to the offering tables. They stood in a line extending across the pavement and toward the stairs coming from the Court of the Gentiles. Others waited their turn just right of the huge bronze laver, its golden sides glowing in the morning sun. Nicky was fascinated watching the priests handle the offerings. Some animals resisted. A goat bleated in protest. One priest silenced the animal with a swift movement of his knife. Smoke curled up from the huge stone altar, and the smell of flesh and incense was both uplifting and sinister. Nicky turned to gaze at the great temple behind the altar. The golden overlay on the towering face reflected the rising sun. The polished white marble carved with flowers and leaves framed the front.

Uncle Joram spoke softly. "Herod, for all his weaknesses, built us a glorious temple. Don't you agree my boy?"

Nicky turned to his uncle. Both he and Nicky's father were dressed in their blue priestly robes. "It's wonderful, Uncle. This is my third time in the temple courts. Last time Father took me to the assembly of the Sanhedrin and I got to listen."

Joram grinned. "And I was with your parents the first time you were here; but I doubt if you, being eight days old, remember well."

Nicky pointed. "Uncle, why is the stone on the big altar so rough? It looks very different from the smooth white temple."

Barak, standing near the two, answered. "Son, do you remember God's instructions to Abraham? He was commanded to use no metal tool on the stone when he built his altars."

Nicky studied his father, admiring his tall, imposing body. Whenever he imagined a temple priest, his father was the image he saw. "But, Father, didn't the Lord also instruct him not to build raised altars—there are five steps on this altar."

Joram chuckled. "Well, Brother, it looks as though your son will some day become a questioning Pharisee like you." He placed his hand on Nicky. "Very good question, young man. Allow me to answer. King Herod followed the Law as long as it didn't interfere with his monumental plans. Often our Law is observed carefully, then other times ..." His voice trailed off. He shook his head.

Barak pointed behind Nicky. "Son, do you see the tower behind that enclosed wall?"

Nicky's eyes followed his father's arm. "Yes, Father."

"And notice it looks over into the temple courtyard?" His voice rose. "And do you see the steps leading down into the outer court, our sacred place of worship?" His voice grew angrier with every word. Turning, he thrust his hand toward the Bronze Gate. "And do you see that image of a golden eagle, the symbol of Rome, above our gate into our very place of meeting with Jehovah?" He clenched his teeth. "That fortress is built to spy on us by King Herod and his Roman soldiers, and that image is a violation of the Law of God—it is a desecration of the Torah." He closed his eyes and breathed deeply.

Nicky felt a sense of pride at his father's words.

Joram's voice was soft as he looked at the rising sun. "My brother has no concept of time—it's a wonder he is so wealthy. Perhaps the rich can afford to make others wait."

Nicky's fingers caressed the scroll on the small stand before him.

Just then, Zedekiah came puffing up the stairs, his fat middle bouncing as he rushed forward. He panted. "I don't know why I trade with these Jerusalem merchants." He turned to Nicky. "Nephew, sorry I'm late. You look great in your new robe." He turned to Barak. "Shall we begin?"

Barak, annoyed, took his place facing Nicky. Uncles flanked Nicky on either side. His bass voice echoed across the marble court. "Hear, O Israel ..."

Nicky heard his father's words, but the spectacle of standing here with the splendor, the smells and the crowd—it almost seemed a dream.

"And now, Nicodemus Joel bar-Barak, as you stand before the congregation of Israel ... upon this holy mount ... in the presence of our mighty God ... do you commit your life to live by his commands?"

Nicky nodded.

Barak acknowledged the nod and went on with preliminaries.

Nicky's mind wandered. His father had to repeat a cue twice before Nicky jolted to reality. His time to stand before the congregation and recite the Torah had come. Nicky's cheeks flushed as he looked as his father, all eyes focused on him.

He lifted the scroll and stood erect. He began with the *shema*: "Hear, O Israel! The Lord is our God, the Lord is one. You shall love the Lord your God with all your heart and with all your soul and with all your might. These words, which I am commanding you today, shall be on your heart. You shall teach them diligently to your sons and shall talk of them when you sit in your house and when you walk by the way and when you lie down and when you rise up. You shall bind them as a sign on your hand and they shall be as frontals on your forehead ..."

Nicodemus dropped the scroll to the stand. There was a murmur from the men. He continued: "You shall write them ..." His memory kicked in. He took a deep breath. This was his moment. A thrill coursed up his spine. His heart throbbed. He raised his hand above his head and his voice echoed from the walls: "When your son asks you in time to come, saying, 'What do the commandments and the statutes and the judgments mean which the Lord commanded you?'"

He recited flawlessly the long, familiar passage and reached the climax. "Therefore, you shall keep the commandment and the statutes and the judgments which I am commanding you today, to do them." He took a deep breath.

All his listeners held their breath.

He emphasized each word. "For you are a holy people to the Lord your God, and the Lord your God has chosen you ..."

A long silence followed after he finished. His father's face showed both pride and amazement. Nicky felt the beads of sweat on his forehead. Even some of the priests ministering near the altar stood in rapt attention.

Finally Barak broke the silence and uttered the *bar 'onshin*. "Blessed be he who has taken the responsibility for this child's doing from me."

Nicky understood the meaning—from this time forward his actions would not be held against his father. Now he was accountable. He was now a man, with all the rights and penalties that accompany this Passage.

The men surged forward. Zedekiah slapped him on the back. "Nicky, from now on I will call you by your full name, Nicodemus. You make our family proud."

As the men led him down the stairs, his mother and the other women all rushed to hug him. Their praises of his recital caused him to blush, but it was pleasant.

Joanna, holding little Jessie, stood back until the confusion died, then she moved beside Nicky and squeezed his arm. "Little brother, I'm proud to be your sister." She kissed him on both cheeks, cocked her head and grinned. "Now let's get something to eat. My arms are about to fall off. My other little brother is heavy."

They headed across the courtyard toward the tall, columned porticos, where long tables of food waited. Many people moved about the crowded porticos flanking the open space. A long reserved table had been covered with white cloths and trays of food.

Nicky hadn't eaten the morning meal. His stomach growled.

Just as they were finding their places, a voice cried, "Barak, Barak, it's happened. Just as I told you it would!"

Everyone turned as two old people hobbled up. The man limped forward, his voice almost a yell, his fist punching the air. "Today it has happened!"

Barak rose; his hands reached toward the frail man. "Simeon, my brother, please come. Sit. What has happened?"

Lips quivering, Simeon exclaimed, "The Lord God has answered my petition—I have seen the one ..." His brow wrinkled and his hands cupped as though holding a precious object. His voice broke. "I held him in these arms. I have seen the Messiah child."

Barak grasped his shoulder. "Where? How did you see this one?"

Simeon, tears in his eyes, sniffed. "Years ago, God spoke to me. He said—The Lord God himself said—I would see the Messiah before I died. Today, a young couple came; the Spirit of Jehovah spoke to me as clearly as we speak today ... 'Go. This child before you now, he is the Chosen One.'" Simeon spoke in hushed tones, his head moving up and down as though he were reciting the Torah.

Barak stroked his cheek, studying Simeon. "So, you say ... your petition has been fulfilled?" His forehead wrinkled, brows arching. He turned to Muriel. "Get some water for these two honored ones." He turned back to Simeon. "You say you saw him, and you know he was the prophesied one?"

Simeon, caught his breath and pointed to Anna. "Tell them, Anna."

The listeners gathered close around the two old people.

Anna began, her voice strained. "I am Anna, daughter of Phanuel. God sent me a prophecy, long years ago, that I would behold the Christ before I die, and today ... " Her voice cracked. "I have seen him." Her tears ran freely. Muriel put an arm around her.

Simeon's wrinkled face was joyous. "Anna has eighty-four years of life. As a prophetess, she has been every day in the temple, waiting." He took her withered hand. "Now we can both rest in peace—the Messiah has come."

Joram asked, "When did you see this child?"

Simeon raised his arms as though in supplication. "A man and a young woman came to offer a pair of pigeons as an offering for their firstborn. The Spirit of God moved me to them."

Anna clasped her hands and affirmed vigorously, "Simeon prophesied. His face glowed like an angel. His voice was strong like a messenger from the throne of God—I will remember his words forever: 'For my eyes have seen your salvation, which you have prepared in the sight of all people, a light for revelation to the Gentiles and for glory to your people Israel.'" She shook her twisted finger. "The young mother listened and when Simeon added words about the child causing the falling and rising of many people, she looked very disturbed. We were so excited, the young parents left before we even found out their names."

Barak helped Simeon to his feet and then knelt before Anna. "God's promises are faithful." He offered his hand to her and she struggled to her feet.

The crowd hushed as Simeon took Anna's arm. They shuffled toward the bronze gate. Nicky watched them pause at the gate, look back at the temple, then disappear into the crowd.

Zedekiah broke the long silence. "Well, this has been one eventful day—may I suggest we eat?"

Barak offered a blessing for their food and Nicodemus was served first. The relatives were gracious with their praises of Nicky, but the whole occasion was subdued, as each pondered the words of the two ancient ones.

Chapter Three

Camels

The sun rose over the Judean hills, chasing away the chill as Nicky descended the worn steps. From inside, he heard the heated debates of his uncles and father. He paused to listen.

Uncle Zedekiah boomed. "But I tell you, Brother, this son of yours has a mind that could bring him great things. I could send him to the Roman school in Caesarea and, with his memory, he could do well in this world."

Nicky moved close to the door. He had never seen Caesarea, never dreamed of attending a Roman school.

Joram interrupted. "You mean be rich and lonely like you?" It was quiet and then Joram, with a gentler voice spoke. "Nicodemus has a mind for the law, and he could follow in his father's footsteps and become a part of the seventy ..."

Muriel who had been mending, cleared her throat loudly.

Zedekiah fired back, "Yes, a part of the mighty Sanhedrin and wear tattered robes, and live in ... " He paused and glanced at Barak, then pleaded, "I only seek the best for a young man of ability. He could live with me during the times of school. My wife would welcome a child in our home."

Barak's voice was firm. "Brother, I do appreciate your offer, but Nicodemus has a desire to attend the temple yeshiva in Jerusalem, where Joram's son attends. Your offer is generous and we thank you, but Muriel and I have only two sons, and Jessie is only a baby. Joanna, I suppose, will soon be married. No, we only have a short time before they will all be gone from our home."

Zedekiah leaned back and exhaled. "Fine, but remember the offer stands. I, too, am proud of a nephew of such a mind. Soon, I would welcome your family to visit Caesarea. Our home is spacious, and we are near the blue ocean. It's beautiful."

Nicodemus pretended not to pay attention. He bounced Jessie on his knee. He longed to see the great ocean.

Muriel punched her brother-in-law playfully. "My son is bright, but at times he can be mischievous, even as you were."

Zedekiah grinned. "Someone's been telling tales."

Just then, there was a rap at the door. Joanna opened it to find Zach, Nicky's friend, excitedly gasping for breath. "Where's Nicky? A bunch of men with camels are at the town well. We need to run quick. The men look rich, and we can earn lots if we beat the others. Those big things will need lots of water."

Both boys raced toward the town well. They were panting by the time they reached the square. The camels were kneeling as the boys grabbed the well covering and began to struggle with the large wooden cover. They had moved the heavy lid only a handbreadth when it was lifted free. A huge, grinning black man laid the large cover beside the well.

He stuck out a massive hand. "I ... servant ... Melchior, Magi of Persia. We pay coin. Need water camel."

The boys tied the bucket to a rope and it splashed into the cool water. They started lugging buckets of water to the nearby trough.

The kneeling camels rose clumsily and moved to drink. Nicky had never watered beasts like these. They slurped the water as quickly as the boys could fill the trough.

Zach muttered, "I don't know how much it will take to fill these things. They drink more than horses or mules."

Nicky sloshed water into the trough. "Yeah, and they smell worse than both put together."

In time, their pace slowed. With the well cover totally removed, Nicky looked into the dark depths of the well. Even though it was bright daylight, he could see the stars reflected from above. He was surprised to see the reflection of the brilliant star he'd seen last week—the night he'd heard the singing. He paused and stared at the star, then hoisted another bucket for the camels.

Sweat dripped from Zach's forehead as he glanced at the richly dressed men watching them. "Where do you suppose these men come from? Don't look like anyone from Judea."

Nicky scratched his cheek, and gazed at the men. Five were in shiny embroidered robes. Their skin was not as dark as their servants'. The black men wore robes of rough brown cloth. All the men wore turbans.

One of the leaders walked toward Nicky. His voice sounded strange. "Boy, I am Melchior, Seer for the Persian King. We seek the new king. King Herod in Jerusalem sent us here to Bethlehem. Where will we find the child-king?"

Nicky froze. Child-king—those were the words of the shepherds. He shook his head. "I don't know. But last week ..." He paused. He didn't know how to explain all that had happened in the last two weeks.

Melchior spoke, his voice deep and resonant. "We followed a great star many miles. We seek the child of that star. Seers in Jerusalem said Bethlehem is the place where he will be born."

Nicky's mind flashed the connection. "The well, the star reflected in the well!" He grasped Melchior's arm and pulled him toward the well. At first, the robed official resisted, but at Nicky's insistence followed him to the well. Nicky pointed down and said, "star." Melchior looked confused but finally bent to look into the depths.

Melchior bolted upright. His eyes were wide. He wheeled to his companions and yelled something sounding like Esther. The men stared at Melchior, slowly moving to join him at the well. Nicky understood nothing they said, but the excitement in their speech was obvious. Melchior pointed down, then to the sky above. The four others frowned and then, one by one, bent to look. With astonished faces, they began jabbering and pointing.

Finally, Melchior took Nicky by the shoulders. His wide smile showed a gold tooth. "This is the star we have followed a long time, across many miles. Now it stands over this very place. Where is this child? Take us to this new King."

Nicky's mind flashed to the temple scene two days before. He didn't know how to explain all that had happened. To his relief, he saw Joanna standing amid the townspeople who had assembled to watch the visitors. He beckoned to her. "Joanna, come."

Melchior watched her closely, but didn't speak.

"Sir, this is my sister." Nicky pointed to the men. "These men have come from the East, they have followed a bright star, and now they want to see the child born to be king ... do you suppose?"

Joanna's mouth dropped open. She gasped. "The singing ... then the shepherds ... now."

Nicky took her hand. "Then at the temple ... Anna and Simeon."

Joanna bowed to Melchior. "Sir, a child was born just ten days past in this town. I don't know where he is now ..." Her face brightened. " ... but my father knows everyone in the town. Perhaps he can find the child for you."

Melchior put the tips of his fingers together. "I will send my men to find food and lodging. I will come to meet your father."

Joanna and Nicky led down the street with Melchior and his black servant following. Once they reached home, Joanna pushed the door open. Their mother, nursing Jessie, gasped at the appearance of the two strangers. She hurriedly put the baby in a basket and brought tea.

The three sat in awkward silence until Barak walked in. He looked puzzled at the appearance of the strangers. Melchior rose and bowed slightly. "Sir, I am Melchior. We have come many days to find a child-king. He was prophesied to be born in Judea. We have journeyed many miles following a star. Today your son has shown us this star. It now stands above your city. We want to find this foretold child-king. Can you help us?"

Barak looked puzzled. "I do not know of such a child. However, we have many who have come from other places in our land to enroll in the Roman census." His hand went to his cheek and he spoke with measured words. "Two days ago, in the temple in Jerusalem, two old prophets claimed a child had been born to fulfill prophesy." His finger touched his lips. "I have a brother who is helping register the descendents of David. He is staying with us, but will not return before sunset. If you come back this evening, we will ask him."

Melchior rose and bowed. "This evening we will return." His servant followed him out and Nicky watched them walk toward the square. His mind was racing. What did all this mean?

*   *   *

At sunset, Joram came in and dropped into a chair. "What a day. We finished Judea and the South. Tomorrow we register those from Galilee and Decapolis and, probably, a few Samaritans."

The meal was dominated by discussion of the strangers who had come from Persia and what their mission could mean.

The dishes were just cleared when a knock sounded. Nicky answered. Five turbaned men dressed in silk stood waiting. Muriel put Jessie in his basket and invited them in. Barak introduced them to Joram.

Joram shook his head when asked about the child. "No one came to register today with a newborn, but we are only part way through the census. Tomorrow more are coming."

Melchior held up his hand. "At morning, I will come to your place of registry." He and his companions bowed, each embracing Barak and Joram as they left.

As the door closed behind them, Joanna turned to her father. "These signs are too strong for denial. What do they mean, Father?"

Barak, his face troubled, shook his head.

Nicky handed his father a coin. "Melchior gave me this coin. It almost looks like gold ... could that be?"

His father took the coin in his teeth and bent it. He studied the imprint. "Gold, solid gold. I don't know the image it bears, but this is gold." He passed it back carefully. "When Zedekiah returns tomorrow, he can determine its value."

*   *   *

Joram had hardly begun the day when a young couple with a child in arms approached his table. The two were from Galilee and the man was a carpenter. The child was named Jesus. After Joram recorded their lineage, he inquired about where they were staying, and said, "I may visit you later, there is a matter we should discuss." He would have asked more, but a line was forming and his day's work lay ahead.

Late in the morning, two men in turbans stood before him. Melchior inquired. "You are Joram, brother to Barak? He told me you are the one who could help me find the promised child. I am Melchior, seer of the King of Persia." He bowed slightly. "Have you found the child born here in Bethlehem?"

Joram checked his book. "A couple, Joseph with his young wife Mary, came within this morning to register. The baby is called Jesus. I wrote the place where they are staying. It is time for my lunch. Come, my brother and I will take you to their place of lodging."

*   *   *

Barak led his whole family down the winding street. They were followed by their turbaned visitors, camels clomping behind. They turned a corner. Barak pointed to a small house near the marketplace. The throng gathered at the door, and after a second knock, a tall broad-shouldered young man answered. He looked surprised, then recognized Joram. "You're the census taker?"

Joram confirmed "I told you I might visit."

The young man wrinkled his brow as he looked at the crowd. "Who?"

A voice from within called, "Joseph, who's there?"

Joseph stepped aside and a young woman holding a baby stood beside him in the doorway. Nicky was surprised: the girl holding the child looked no older than his sister.

25

"Joseph, who are all these people?" she asked.

Barak spoke. "My brother tells me you are Joseph and Mary from Nazareth, and you have just borne a son whom you named Jesus. This is correct?"

"This is true, but why?"

Melchior stepped forward. "Young woman, we have come far. We come following star of new king. We wish to worship this one, the one born to be new king."

The other robed men moved forward. Melchior bowed. "We bring gifts for baby king."

At first, Mary looked astonished. Then a look of understanding crossed her face. "Our house is small but ... come in." She looked around the room, then at the group of people at her door. "Or as many as can fit."

Nicky and Joanna were the last to squeeze into the tiny space. Several servants of the Magi pushed forward carrying gifts. Melchior was the only one of the visitors who spoke Aramaic, but the others nodded at his words. Mary sat in a low chair, the baby in her lap. The strangers bowed in reverence. One by one, the men knelt and presented gifts, opening them before Mary and the baby.

Melchior opened a bag. "This gold is of Persia ..." He took an ornamented vase. "This is nard, a royal aroma for a king." Another servant set two heavy bags before Mary. "This frankincense ... this myrrh."

Mary clasped her hands together, her eyes sparkled. "We thank you. Our child has been well heralded by God. Many others have foretold us of God's plan for him. Joseph and I are humbled and honored that you have come to confirm what has been prophesied."

Melchior stood and placed his hands on Joseph's shoulders. "Now to the father of this one who is born a king, I have a message from above." He pointed upward. "Last night as I slept, a holy one came to me, He wore bright clothing. He spoke these words: 'Herod will try to find this child and kill him.' We must leave this night. King Herod will not be happy with us."

Mary uttered a little cry and clutched the baby to her.

Joseph enclosed Mary in his arms. "You leave tonight ... but we—"

Melchior's face showed his concern. "God has given you a special task. Often with great honors come great trials. This child is one who will bring many changes to your land. We must go before Herod finds us." The Magi rose, and within a short time Nicodemus could hear the clomp of the camels moving down the street.

*   *   *

That night the bright star still illuminated their rooftop. Nicky lay awake for a long time, thinking about all he'd seen. His eyes grew heavy. He finally dropped off to sleep.

Joanna shook him awake. The moon was gone from the sky. "Nicky, someone is here." Joanna was already to the stairs when Nicky kicked into his sandals and followed his sister. At the front door, he saw his whole family huddled around Mary and the baby. Joseph held the rope to their little donkey which was loaded heavily for a long journey.

Joseph embraced Mary. "Tonight, I had just dropped to sleep when an angel of God appeared and awakened me. He told me that we had to leave tonight for Egypt. King Herod wants to kill our child."

Zedekiah exclaimed, "An angel? You saw an angel?"

"It was the same angel that appeared while we were in Nazareth, the one who spoke of this miraculous birth." Joseph grabbed Barak's shoulder. "We must flee to Egypt tonight ... that is what the angel said. I packed as quickly as I could, but our little donkey is almost lame. He cannot carry these gifts the men from the East gave us. These gifts are too heavy. We need to leave. My wife cannot travel on foot."

Muriel put her arm about Mary.

Zedekiah stroked the little donkey and then turned to Joseph. His finger tapped his lips. "Young man, I think I have a deal ... a deal you can't refuse. Suppose I trade your donkey for my mule. He's twice the size of this little beast. He is around in back." He turned to his nephew. "Nicky, go fetch my mule. Put my bridle and saddle on him." He turned to face Mary. "You two can bring him back when you return to this land."

Joseph merely looked from face to face.

Zedekiah pointed upward. "I know the route to Egypt well and several places along the way that will treat you kindly. At Beersheba ..." He withdrew a tablet from his robe and scribbled a rough map. He continued, "Now in Gaza, at the Inn of the Seven Rams, Berikiah is the innkeeper and he will care for you. Tell him you are my friend. He is honest and he will instruct you on the best routes into Egypt." He scribbled more instructions.

Nicodemus led the mule onto the street.

Joseph examined the beast. "This animal is worth five donkeys. Could I pay—?"

Zedekiah raised his palm. Let's say this is my investment in our new king. Keep your coins, you will need them."

Joanna whispered to Nicodemus, "That mule is his pride and joy."

Zedekiah grinned. "Besides, everyone thinks I need to walk more."

Barak knelt before Mary. "If you like, I will keep your spices as a sacred trust until it is safe for you to return to this land. It is only fitting a king be anointed with frankincense and myrrh."

Joseph took three gold coins and tried to give them to the brothers, but they shook their heads. Zedekiah spoke for all. "We will not take your gold. This is meant for greater needs."

Nicky whispered to his sister, "Isn't frankincense used for funerals?"

Chapter-Four

Terror

Nicky didn't know what awakened him. He sat up and looked around the room. His brother slept quietly in the little basket. The rest of the house was still. Then he heard what sounded like a wail coming from outside. The sound grew louder. He saw a light from beyond the curtain to his room. Someone else had heard the cry. Pushing the drape aside he saw, in the flickering olive oil light, both his parents standing by the door. Another wail echoed through the window and Joanna rushed in. She and her mother clung to each other. Nicky moved closer.

"Mother, it's someone screaming," Joanna whispered. Barak pulled on his heavy cloak. With his brothers and their families gone, only the five of them remained. Another wail sounded even closer, then a sudden banging shook their door.

"Open by the order of King Herod," a voice barked. Barak started to open the door when it was blasted open by a Roman boot. There were four soldiers, two with their short swords drawn. The youngest among them, the one with an unusually big nose, held a flaming torch.

Nicky felt a chill. He stared at the Roman short sword, the one famous for subduing every nation that dared challenge Rome. He remembered their motto: "Never draw your sword unless you plan to use it." One of the swords was covered with blood.

The oldest soldier held a parchment in his fist. He glared at Nicky's father. "Your name is Barak and your wife is Muriel. Is this correct?"

Barak squared his shoulders. "That is my name, what is your business?" One of the soldiers put the tip of his sword to Barak's throat. The point caused a small trickle of red to run down his neck. "I do not wish to kill you, but that remains your decision. Where is your son?"

Nicky felt his heart stop. Both women recoiled as the older soldier glanced his way.

"Not that one. A baby."

Muriel paled as one of the soldiers pushed the curtain aside leading to the boys' sleeping-room. He pointed with his sword. "In here."

The soldier with the bloody sword strode into the room, followed by the torch bearer. A moment later, they returned holding Jessie like a bag of grain. The soldier ripped the cloth gown away and Jessie yelled in protest.

The leader of the men snarled, "It's a boy."

Muriel screamed as a soldier thrust his sword into the infant's abdomen. The blade slashed upward into his chest. Jessie's scream ended in a bloody gurgle as he plopped to the floor.

Nicky felt as though his heart had stopped. He watched Jessie flail his little arms, quiver, and then, lie motionless. A scream caught in his throat. He glanced at the torch bearer, the one with the large nose, as a tear ran down his cheek.

The older soldier wiped his sword on the baby's rent gown and threw it over Jessie's contorted body. Then the soldiers were gone and Jessie lay crumpled in a growing pool of red. Nicky stood frozen. Barak mutely held his sobbing wife. She tore from his grip, ran to Jessie, and fell prostrate over his body.

Nicky stared at his sister in the dim light. Tears were on her cheek, but her jaw was clenched, muscles in her cheeks bulging. He had never before seen such a look of hatred on her face.

He almost didn't recognize her icy voice. "I despise Romans, I wish them all dead." She knotted her fists. "I vow, before my God ... I will remember those faces, I will never, never forget."

Barak touched his daughter.

She pulled away. "You just stood there while they killed him ... You just stood!"

Time stopped as she glared at her father.

Nicky cried, "Joanna, Father had a sword at his throat. Did you want him dead, too?"

Joanna moaned. "We're all dead. We Jews are all dead."

* * *

That night in Bethlehem, ancient Ramah, twenty-three boys under the age of two were put to death. The whole city wailed. The days were dark as one burial followed another. The prophecy of Jeremiah was fulfilled: "A voice is heard in Ramah, mourning and great weeping. Rachel weeping for her children and refusing to be comforted, because the children are no more."

* * *

Life seemed to go out of Muriel. She moved about the house like a ghost. Her soft singing was gone. Nicky often heard her weeping at night, but it was Joanna who had, in that awful moment, changed the most. Her sweet disposition was hardened in one brutal night. She became abrupt, her ready smile gone.

One night, Nicky heard Barak talking to his daughter. He crept to the curtain to listen.

"My daughter, a vow is not to be taken lightly. You can be absolved since it was in a time—"

"My vow I will keep. I hate these cursed Romans. I will avenge the senseless murders. I curse Rome."

"My daughter, you must not curse. Hatred is a bad thing; it will eat your very heart. You must—"

She cut him off. "How long will we tolerate killing of infants? How long does the Torah tell us to allow wicked men to kill innocent babies?" Her voice was almost a scream. "Tell me, my father, how long?"

Nicky crept from the curtain. He'd never heard his sister being rude to Father. He was glad to be going to the yeshiva in Jerusalem in three weeks. Their home was so changed. He wondered—forever?

*   *   *

The night of terror was two weeks past. Joanna waited for the rest of the family to go to bed. She listened carefully. All was quiet. She fastened her heavy cloak about her and pulled the hood to cover her head. Carrying her sandals to avoid sound, she stole to the door.

A soft voice caused her to freeze. "Joanna, where are you going?"

She turned.

Nicky stood behind her.

"I thought you were asleep. I just had someone to see, and I needed ..." She searched for an explanation.

"Would Father approve?"

Joanna felt her anger rise. "I am sixteen, and I do not need to have my father check on everyone I see." She quieted. "Please don't wake them. I'll only be gone for a little bit, I have a friend waiting ..."

"I won't tell ... be careful ... . You and Dory can get in trouble. The soldiers are still roaming the streets."

Joanna felt a gush of relief. Nicky assumed she was meeting with Dory from next door. "Thank you, you're a nice brother to have around." She ruffled his hair.

She slipped into her sandals and walked out. A male voice whispered from the shadows, "We have to hurry; the meeting will already have begun."

Chapter Five

Yeshiva

Nicky slid into the seat beside his cousin Joseph. This was the fifth week of his acceptance into the Jerusalem yeshiva. He glanced at the crowded shelves of scrolls below the four glass windows. Probably few schools in all the country had real glass like these. On the opposite side, quotations covered the wall. Six straight lines of chairs faced the desk at the front. The room was almost filled. Nicky caught the amused glances of other boys. Being the youngest in the class was uncomfortable.

A fourth-year student named Caiaphas turned and sneered. "Well, I see Joseph of Arimathea escorted his quiet little friend again today."

Joseph glared back at Caiaphas. He whispered to Nicky, "Pay no attention. He thinks his curly locks disguise his lack of brains."

Gamaliel, the teacher for the afternoon session, strode into the room. He looked around the class and smacked his right fist into his palm. He slowly studied the assembled boys. "Good afternoon, my Torah scholars."

Joseph nudged Nicky. "Watch, he's doing his thing."

Gamaliel stroked his chin. "And now, young academians, I have a question for today."

Joseph whispered, "And now, he baits his hook."

"If we look into the writings of the patriarch Job ..." Gamaliel opened a worn scroll, taking his time to find the place—even though the whole class knew he could recite it from memory—"Ahh, here it is." His palm rose. "If a man dies shall he live again?" He placed the scroll on his desk and pursed his lips. "Now, my young scholars, what do you think?"

The first to respond was Caiaphas. He stood and stated emphatically, "My father says—"

Gamaliel interrupted. "Young man, I didn't inquire about your father's position. I asked for your original thoughts." His eyes twinkled under heavy brows. "Perhaps you would share your own thoughts on the subject."

Caiaphas slumped to his seat. After a period of silence, Gamaliel strode across the room. He opened his palms to invite response, his eyes searching.

Finally one student near the rear timidly raised his hand. "I have read that Rabbi Hillel stated that there is life after death."

"And how do you suppose the learned rabbi reached that conclusion?"

For the next hour more students responded, with Gamaliel asking penetrating questions. Often his comments were humorous, but he didn't take sides in the controversy. Finally, near the end of class, he asked, "How many of you affirm a belief in eternal life? Indicate by raising your hand." The class was almost evenly divided.

Gamaliel looked carefully at each face, both index fingers pointing to the class. "In our next session, I want you to sit on the right side of the room if you affirm a belief in an afterlife, and if you do not believe there is life after death, you will sit on the left. You may ask your father's position and that may affect your decision. You have this evening to think it over, but I will ask you to defend your beliefs." He lifted his eyebrows. "Class dismissed."

Joseph and Nicky bounded down the steps leading from the temple platform. "My father says that all good people will live with God." Joseph ventured. "I just didn't want to have to be questioned by the teacher. He can be really tough. Your father ever talk about it?"

"He's pretty much the same, but they are brothers."

They turned into the narrow street leading to the marketplace. It was market day and the narrow lanes were crowded with merchants and buyers haggling over prices. Nicky loved the colorful piles of goods and the banter of the vendors. The aroma of roasting lamb and honey cakes blended with the smell of spices. The stalls with woolen garments, olive wood carvings were tucked in among sellers of jade and ivory. Merchants selling brass pots and live animals were on the far end. He headed toward a familiar fruit stand piled high with apples, oranges, lemons and vegetables. He spotted the girl he was looking for serving other customers. He didn't know her name yet, but she had long braided hair, a bright smile and sparkling green eyes. She wore a blue and gold dress. A silver coin dangled on her forehead.

She grinned when she saw him waiting. He pointed to the red apples at her elbow. "I'll take two of those."

She carefully selected two, and rubbed them to a bright sheen. As she handed them across the table, her fingers stroked his, and she leaned closer. "They're very good. I'm glad you buy them from me. That will be two brass shekels. We have other good things too if you are interested." Her voice had a lilting sound. She winked.

Nicky wanted to ask her name but his face flushed just thinking about it.

As they moved through the crowd, Joseph chuckled. "She over charged you, you know. Be careful, cousin. She's older, and much wiser." He punched Nicky on the arm. "Come on, our house mother will not be pleased if we are not at studies by the sixth hour."

Nicky passed an apple to Joseph, and hoped his cousin couldn't hear his beating heart. Joseph would just tease him. A large bunch of students from the upper level of their yeshiva stood in the lane ahead. Their presence distracted Nicky from his thoughts about the fruit seller.

Joseph pulled Nicky into a doorway and pointed. "I know those boys from school. Those two men in the center are Matthias bar-Eliach and Judah bar-Shragai. They're teachers of the advanced students."

Nicky sensed the excitement of the students. He strained to hear Matthias speak.

"And what do you think, young men of the nation of Abraham? Our law states we should make no images of men or beasts. Now, above our very temple gate the Romans have placed a golden eagle." There was a rumble of dissent. "Why do you suppose they do this?" His fist raised to the sky: "To remind us of our slavery?"

Someone in the crowd shouted, "Tear it down!" The murmur spread among the students. "Rip it from our gates!" Another voice yelled, "We should die rather than profane God's temple!"

The other rabbi cautioned, "Quiet, we must quiet ourselves. What we may do must not be known by our oppressors."

Joseph pulled Nicky back into the street, his face troubled. "We need to get to our boarding room. We're already late." Nicky looked back at the students. They had pulled into a tight circle, but he could hear their excited chatter. Something was about to happen, he wished he knew what.

*   *   *

The next day, as Nicky arrived at class, other students were moving to new seats dependent on their answer to the teacher's question. Nicky and Joseph were on the right, those who believed in an afterlife.

Gamaliel strode into class and looked around the divided class. "Today my scholars, our session will be short. In one hour, I will be meeting with many of your fathers as the Sanhedrin assembles. This is one of the many unscheduled gatherings that clutter the life of adults. For today's discussion, I see you have divided as I instructed. May I pose my question? First, to those on my right. How many of your fathers are Pharisees, those that believe in life after death?"

Nicky was surprised; every boy on his side of the room raised his hand.

Gamaliel turned to the others. "And I suppose that on this side all of your fathers are of the Sadducee's persuasion?"

One tall student rose to his feet. "Teacher, my father is neither. Matters of eternity do not concern him. What matters are the horrid woes thrust upon our nation by Herod and his Roman masters."

Gamaliel exclaimed, "Ah, and we have a Zealot among us." He did his palms up gesture. "And so we have young Jews who have already assimilated their father's belief system. All right, let's see who can logically defend these beliefs."

There was a protracted silence and finally Nicky timidly raised his hand.

Gamaliel indicated for Nicky to stand. "Now our youngest member, one of the Pharisees' camp, ventures his opinion."

Nicky gulped. "In the Psalms of David, in his shepherd's psalm, the final words are, 'and I shall dwell in the house of the Lord forever.'" He started to sit, but Gamaliel indicated he remain standing.

The teacher walked toward Nicky. "And now for the first time in our discussion of eternal life, our new member is the first to quote from the sacred writings. May I commend you." He turned to the others. "What do the words 'dwell forever' mean? Can any of you, from our law, poetry or prophets, answer this young man?"

There was another time of embarrassing silence.

Gamaliel continued, "As most of you know, I am a Pharisee, and I am a believer that our God sent us a law that should govern our lives. Yes, I believe he sent the ten plagues and opened the sea to allow our fathers to pass through to freedom. I believe he controls what he will, to his glory."

Caiaphas stood, and was recognized. "If Jehovah is so all-powerful, why does he allow things like the massacre at Bethlehem to happen?"

"Good question." Gamaliel turned to the right side of the room. "Does anyone on this side of the room have an answer?"

After another protracted silence, Nicky rose. Gamaliel raise an eyebrow. "You, Nicodemus, are the son of Barak of Bethlehem, is this correct?"

Nicky dropped his chin.

The teacher spoke softly. "In our meeting of the seventy last week, our condolences went to your father and family for the loss of your little brother. I respect your father and family. I know you have faced this question, what is your answer?"

Nicky felt his eyes grow moist. "May I state my father's belief ... which I also hold?"

The teacher lifted his palm in permission.

"My father says, 'Though God is all powerful, a force of evil is in this world." He gulped. " ... A force of evil that took the life of my brother. God gives men the ability to decide. Often they choose wicked deeds." Nicky dropped to his seat.

Gamaliel stroked his beard, then he pointed upward. "Free will, a blessing ... and, at times a curse." The silence in the room was thick. "And now class, I want you to open your minds to what God spoke through the prophet Moses."

Suddenly, the door burst open, and Rabbi Samuel rushed in. "I'm sorry to interrupt your class, but I must talk to you." He rushed to Gamaliel's side and whispered in his ear.

Nicky could only hear part of the conversation, but he heard Gamaliel blurt—"Twenty members of the Sanhedrin? When?" Then he heard, "Taken prisoner?"

The whole class sat forward. "Prisoners? Do you have a list?"

Gamaliel turned to the class, his face pale. "How many in this class have fathers who are members of the Council of the Seventy?"

A fearful silence filled the room like a winter blast. Many of the students from both sides slowly lifted their hands.

Gamaliel spoke, his face tight with fear. "Rabbi Samuel brings alarming news." He paced. "As the Sanhedrin assembled, Roman soldiers, sent from Herod arrested the following men." He turned to Rabbi Samuel.

Rabbi Samuel pulled a scrawled list from his pocket. He read, "Shamiel of Jerusalem, Barsimon of Hebron ..."

As he continued, Nicky felt his throat tighten. Several students cried out as their fathers' names were read. Near the end of the list Rabbi Samuel intoned, "Barak of Bethlehem." and Nicky felt his whole world begin to spin.

Nicky's head dropped to his desk. His tears flowed freely. There were other noises around him but his mind tumbled. "First little Jessie, now Father." He felt Joseph's hand on his shoulder. Through his fear he blurted, "Why? Why?"

Joseph helped him to his feet. "Come on, Nicky, my father's name wasn't read. We'll find him. Perhaps he can tell us more. I only hope there was no mistake and he wasn't taken too."

The boys pushed to the door.

Gamaliel joined them. "I think I know where Joram will be. Follow me, boys."

Gamaliel led the two, his stride long and quick. He rushed into the back courts and through a series of twisting tunnels. The boys were panting as the teacher pushed open a heavy door to a lower chamber.

Nicky looked around the room. Anxious eyes stared at them. He recognized several of the men as priests, friends of his father. His eyes searched for Barak and, in the process, he saw his uncle Joram slumped in the corner. Nicky whispered, "Joseph, there's your father."

Joseph ran to Joram.

Nicky's gaze again searched the faces of the assembled men. Perhaps the list of names was wrong. Each set of eyes sent a spear deeper into his heart. Barak was not there.

He slumped toward his uncle Joram, who took him in his arms. "All we know is that the centurion had a list, and they came and took them away."

Gamaliel sat beside Joram and the boys. "We do know that Herod once said that when he dies he wants weeping in Judea."

Joram gulped. "And our informants tell us, Herod is in Jericho, near death."

Gamaliel put his arm around Nicky, and turned to Joram. "Will you take Nicodemus to Bethlehem? I know Barak is your brother. You'd be the best one to bring the news of his arrest to the family."

Joram rose heavily. The boys followed to the door leading up to the temple.

Nicky's feet dragged down the crowded streets. The busy market held no interest. Nor did the fruit stand girl who watched him slump by. Joram led them out the gate and into the Kidron Valley.

As they passed an old olive tree, now sprouting new foliage, Joram spotted a fellow scribe slumped on a bench. "Zadok, did you heard the news? Members of the Sanhedrin have been taken as prisoners."

The old man looked up, his eyes troubled. "I know, only an hour past, a Roman troop marched by here with a long line of our most respected men—tied together like cattle."

Joram fell to his knees before the old man. "Where will they be taken?"

The old man sniffed. "The centurion I know, he spoke to me. They were taking them to the Hasmonean Palace outside Jericho. That's all he said." His head dropped to his chest, and he muttered, "Herod plans to kill the leaders of our nation ... so there will be weeping at his death."

Chapter Six

Herod

It was near dark when Joseph, Joram, and Nicky reached Bethlehem. Nicky opened the door to find Muriel and Joanna in heated discussion.

Muriel moaned, "But Joanna, your hair was so beautiful. Now you look like a boy."

"If I choose to cut my hair, it's my choice. If only I was a boy—and had a sword."

Joram cleared his throat and both women turned, surprise creasing their faces. Muriel stared at the three, a puzzled look on her face. "Nicky, why are you here? I thought you'd be in Jerusalem ... and Joram, and Joseph?"

Nicky started to speak but the startled look on his mother's face made him stop. Joram walked to Muriel and placed his palm on her shoulder. "Please stay seated. The news I bear is difficult. Barak and a large number of the Seventy have been taken by Herod's soldiers."

Muriel, fingers spread wide, grasped her face. A wail escaped her lips. "How could? He was in a meeting ... The Sanhedrin, it just assembled ..."

Joanna covered her mouth. "Father? They arrested Father?"

Joram pulled up a stool and faced the women. "We know little of the reasons." He clasped his fingers and slowly shook his head.

Joseph, biting his lip, added. "Herod's near death and they say he wants Jews to weep at his funeral."

Joram interrupted. "It just happened, only a short time past. We came to inform you. At the present we can only pray. Our God is good ..."

Joanna stomped her foot. "Perhaps God is waiting for us to quit praying and take action."

Nicky watched her face. Her teeth clenched. Sparks filled her eyes. With her hair cut short and hatred on her face, she reminded him of the students in the street, those called Zealots.

* * *

That Sabbath day, their worship at the synagogue was hollow. Without Barak presiding, the whole assembled congregation was dealt a sickening blow. Later, back at home, Nicky could barely offer the blessing for their Shabbat meal.

It was the first day of the week when Nicky returned with his cousin and uncle to Jerusalem. Entering the gates to the city, they sensed an eerie tension.

Joram pulled aside a passerby to inquire. "Why is the city so quiet?"

The man glanced around. "You didn't hear? Thursday evening a mob of students took axes to the eagle atop the Beautiful Gate and chopped it down. Forty of them were arrested and King Herod has returned from Jericho—as sick as he is—to try them. The trial is today." He glanced furtively around. "I'd better not say more ...it's a bad time ... soldiers in every street." He scurried away.

Joram thought for only a moment. "If they are tried, it will be in the Roman Praetorium. Come, I know a shortcut. We'll need to stand in the outer courtyard, but I am known by Herod's servants. No one will bother us. Both you boys need to see what's happening, and I must know. The rabbis who lead this band of young Zealots are members of the Seventy."

Nicky and his cousin followed Joram as he scurried down the back streets to the west section of the old city. When they arrived, a crowd was already assembling outside the gate. Joram and the two boys were admitted by a servant. They found a place to observe the trial from behind a row of plants. From their hidden place they saw guards surrounding the students. The young men were sitting cross-legged on the pavement, wrists bound behind them.

It was mid-day when Herod, face flushed with fever, entered the Praetorium on a litter. The forty students, most members of the yeshiva's advanced class, were already sweating in the heat. They sat erect and defiant as Herod was carried to the raised platform before the inner doors to the palace. He frowned at the prisoners.

Herod sat up from his position on the litter. He winced as his feet touched the pavement. He listened as charges were read. Squinting at the students he demanded, "Who told you to do this? Why would you destroy the eagle from the gate?"

One young man thundered, "The Law of our Fathers. You have desecrated our holy place. You have violated the Law of our God. We have obeyed God and cut that idol from our temple gate!"

Herod grimaced as he glared at the line of boys, his face contorted. "Why are you so cheerful? Do you realize, even now execution fires are being built in the Hinnom Valley?"

Another shouted, "Because, after death, we shall enjoy greater blessings!"

Herod's body trembled as he raised his hand to the centurion. "These young men, by their own admission, are guilty! By their choice—" His voice cracked. "—they will be burnt to death before the sun sets this day." His fist was shaking, then he slumped to the litter. He moaned. "Our judgment seat is closed."

Nicky watched in awe and terror as the students were jerked to their feet. The young men who were his upper-classmates were being led to painful death. He watched their faces—many he knew by name. They held their heads high. Didn't they realize?

Joram pushed back into the shrubs and pulled the two boys with him. The crowd attending the trial filed past. Looks of shock and disbelief covered their faces.

Nicky watched as a cordon of soldiers pushed the remaining Jews aside.

"Make way for the king. Move back!"

He stared into the litter that carried Herod. The king's face was pock-marked and discolored. Herod doubled over, moaning, his fingers scratching sores on his face. Was this wretched old man really the great builder of Caesarea, the walls of Jerusalem, the glorious temple? He looked more miserable than the beggars at the Dung Gate.

Nicky remembered the story from Jeremiah about the Hinnom Valley. It was the place where the pagans offered their children to the fires of Molech—the reason the Jewish word for eternal punishment is *gehenna.* He never thought he'd experience hearing the screams of youths being burned to death outside his beloved city—the city of Jerusalem. A shudder raced through his body. The name Jerusalem—it was supposed to mean *peace of the Jews.*

*   *   *

Salome fanned herself. Jericho in the spring was hot, and even the groves Herod had planted brought little cooling. These three days, with her brother away in Jerusalem, had brought some comfort. The palace gardens did cool a little in the evenings. Being far below sea-level, Jericho was seldom cold, and too often like a furnace. They'd have deserted this Dead Sea palace if it had not been for the king's worsening health. At first the hot baths had led to some relief for his putrefying body. With his murders of his wife and three sons, Herod was a lonely old man. She consoled herself—as his sister, she was his only true source of companionship. It gave her great power which she relished, but at times, when he was delirious, she wished he was dead. He smelled of death. His end had been long delayed too long.

The trumpet at the gates signaled her little respite was gone. Herod had returned. The household servants rushed to meet his litter and he was carried into the large courtyard.

Salome reached and took his hand. He was shivering in the heat. "Does my brother want something to eat?"

Herod opened his eyes. "Ah, my sister ... " He raised a shaky palm to the servants. "No food, just something to drink."

The servants brought several beverages but Herod took only water. His eyes stared beyond the trellised ceiling. "I have just seen forty young men who gladly faced death .to defy Rome. I just don't understand it. They could have pled ..."

Salome tried to distract him. "Tonight my brother a play in our theater, and—"

Herod raised a hand. "Why? Why would they cut down the eagle?" He gulped the water and coughed. "I have built them a beautiful temple, the finest in the world ... why?"

Salome tried again. "The sums you allocated to your soldiers were distributed, and the legion hailed your generosity. It took the treasury of two storehouses, but you will be long remembered."

Herod glared at her, his voice rasping. "Have my orders been given to the troops concerning these captives?" His arm pointed downhill to the stadium. "About these leaders of this stubborn race?"

Salome stiffened; his mind had still not forgotten his planned vengeance on the Jewish nation. "The centurions have been given the order that if you die—"

"Not if ... it is not if. I am dying! My body is rotting, I am dying!" He was seized by violent coughing. When he recovered he clutched her sleeve. "Upon my death, these Jewish leaders now held in the Hippodrome are to be killed."

Salome was surprised by the strength of his grip.

"They are to be killed, and then all these accursed Jews throughout this land will weep. This nation will mourn when the great King Herod dies."

Herod dropped back on the couch and Salome pointed to his bed chamber. The servants moved him to his room. It wouldn't be long ... But she had thought that before.

* * *

Two days later Salome entered the King's bed chamber. There was a rancid smell. His body was cold. She stared at the brother who had built so much, conquered great cities, and been such a skilled politician. Her fingers trembled as she slowly closed his eyes.

Salome straightened, tightening her robe around her. She pulled the cord to summon the servants. When they came, she ordered, "Send for the centurion."

While she waited she started her letter to Rome. Shortly, she heard the clomping of boots as the officer entered the chamber and saluted. She rose, her voice decisive. "I have this final request from King Herod." She leveled her gaze into the waiting centurion's eyes. "All the prisoners are to be released immediately. This is the last wish of King Herod."

Chapter Seven

Caesarea

Nicodemus felt all bubbly inside. His father walked ahead of Joanna and Muriel, the sun warm on their shoulders. Even the little donkey seemed happy with his light load, mincing down the roadway beside Barak. Ahead, the roadway was full of people coming up the hill bringing goods of all description to Jerusalem. A string of donkeys so heavily loaded they looked like moving haystacks with legs carried giant jars that smelled of palm oil. A cart with creaking wheels was piled high with brightly colored garments.

On the horizon, the cities of the Plains of Sharon dotted the bursting green meadows. In the distance, Nicodemus could see the blue ocean. The soft breeze brought a slight smell of sea.

Barak tugged the little donkey away from the tall grasses on the bank. Ahead were the houses of Lydda. He turned. "Muriel, are you sure you don't want to ride for a while?" He watched her as she ambled behind.

She shook her uncombed head, her face tired, eyes listless. "How long will it take us to reach Caesarea?"

Joanna whispered to Nicky, "I'm glad Father decided to take us to see Uncle Zedekiah. Mother had to get away from Bethlehem and the memories."

Nicky jerked a leaf from the low branches beside the road. "And, I'm glad we finally get to visit Uncle. I really want to swim in the ocean."

"My brother, neither you nor I have ever been swimming."

Nicky swatted at a bee. "But I've read about it, and I think I can do it."

Joanna gave him a pained look and moved beside her mother. "Isn't it a beautiful day, Mother? Look at all these flowers beside the road." She plucked one and held it to her mother's face—no response. She withdrew it.

Muriel just plodded on.

Nicky joined his father. His throat tightened as he glanced at the rope burns on Barak's wrist. "Did the Romans beat you when they took you to Jericho?"

Barak handed the donkey's rope to his son. "No, Nicodemus. In fact, the soldiers treated us kindly. Yes, we were tied together to prevent escape, but once we reached Jericho they put us in the Hippodrome. They gave us water and we were fed once a day. The food, though plain, was not bad."

"You don't hate them?"

"None of the soldiers wanted to harm us. It was only Herod who wanted us killed. Remember, Son, it was his very own sister who released us. The soldiers even gave us food for our journey to Jerusalem. No, my son, I don't hate the Romans. In fact, the weight I lost during those weeks was probably of benefit. That time has made me appreciate things much more."

"What things, Father?"

Barak stroked the donkey's neck. "Things like my family" His jaw clenched. "Even though we all miss little Jessie." He glanced back at his wife. "I also appreciate my freedom and that the Sanhedrin is still free to rule our people." He took the rope from Nicky and pulled the donkey back to the path. "This is a great day, and God has given it to us to be thankful." He pointed to a road that led to the left. "Down that road is the town of Zorah. Do you remember the warrior who came from there?"

Nicky shook his head.

"He was one of the greatest fighters of our history. He would have made the athletes of Greece look weak and slow."

"David didn't come from Zorah."

"No, not David." Father chuckled. "That warrior was from our town of Bethlehem. Come now; who was the fighter who put the gates of a city on his shoulders, then carried them to the top of a hill twenty-miles away? The one who caught foxes and tied their tails together to burn the Philistines' crops?"

Nicky's face lit up. "And pushed the pillars down on the heathens ... Samson!" He frowned at his father. "He was from Zorah?"

His father's voice was solemn. "Yes, the man who could have done so much for his people ... and was their biggest disappointment ..."

"Why do you say that?"

Barak patted the little donkey's head. "Sampson could have liberated his people. He had a body stronger and faster than any man, yet he spent the time in seeking pleasure and revenge."

"But he killed many Philistines."

"Yes, and he ended his life blind, a chained slave, and in suicide. God planned for him to bring deliverance, and it took a shepherd of Bethlehem to finish the job of subduing the Philistines."

"You mean King David?"

Barak's head tilted. "You are correct my son. It took a man after God's own heart."

They were nearing the town when Barak turned to the women. "We will spend the night here in Lydda, and tomorrow continue on. I have a friend who will welcome us here. He too, was one of the captives at Jericho."

After reaching the place of lodging, Nicky took the donkey to the stable behind the house, where he found grain and water. Nicky rubbed the donkey's neck. Turning to leave, he felt the soft nose of the animal push against his back. He looked into its big brown eyes. He spotted a brush beside the crib, retrieved it and gently stroked the donkey's long neck. He heard a sound behind him and turned to Barak who had quietly entered the shed.

"Good evening, Father."

"I was wondering what delayed you. You looked deep in thought."

"Father, last night when we were on our roof in Bethlehem and we saw the lights from Herodium and heard the trumpets ..."

"We all heard them, Son. Herod's funeral was a big affair. It was a great display, the biggest funeral procession our nation has ever seen." He took the brush from his son and brushed the donkey's other side. "But, what was missing?"

"What do you mean?"

"The sound of wailing, my son ... the sound of people crying. No one wept to see the greatest builder of our times dead. Even his soldiers were glad to see King Herod gone." Barak replaced the brush on the shelf and put his arm around his son. "Can you imagine a future king being carried by such a small beast as this? Come, our host has prepared food. Tomorrow we will have a long journey."

*   *   *

The next day, the four traveled up the Sharon Valley. Farmers worked the fields and the trees were filled with birds. The smell of apple blossoms filled the air. Muriel's steps were a little lighter and Nicky hummed a little tune. This was the longest time he had spent with his father.

"Father, the donkey isn't limping as much. Do you think Uncle will keep him?"

"My son, I doubt very much if Zedekiah was very interested in this beast. His exchange was for the benefit of Joseph of Nazareth, his wife, and child. No, this little donkey is of little value. My brother was only being generous."

"Father, now that Herod is dead, will this child of the star return?"

Barak looked thoughtful. "We have long awaited a messiah ... a long, long time. Someday, you will probably live to find that answer."

The women joined them. Joanna sounded agitated. "There are certainly many Roman troops on this road."

"Do you still hate them?" Barak studied his daughter. In spite of her short hair, she still had a woman's face.

"I will always hate those that killed Jessie."

Barak said nothing but stared at her wrinkled forehead.

"Someday ...maybe soon, I hope you learn to forgive. For this short time let us enjoy our time together." They wound their way through a band of sheep that were freshly shorn. One shepherd led the flock and a young one followed with his dog. None seemed in any hurry, except the men with loaded donkeys following.

They had just passed a small grove of trees when a voice from behind them ordered, "Jew, you have a beast and I have a heavy pack. I require that you carry it for me."

Barak turned to face two Roman soldiers. He pulled the beast to a halt and the soldier placed his pack on the donkey. Barak helped him tie the pack securely. Hardly a word was exchanged. Still, Nicky noticed Joanna was clenching her fists.

Nicky studied the soldiers; they looked tired. They were about the age of his father and they spoke a language he didn't understand. They wore their helmets, but no chain armor or greaves on their legs. Approaching Joppa, one soldier took the pack and without a word, marched off down the road.

Nicky watched his father. "He didn't even thank you."

"No son, he didn't. Often in life, good deeds are rewarded by God alone."

*   *   *

On the third day of the journey, they approached Caesarea. Zedekiah's home was located on a small rise south of the city gates. He was in the yard and saw the four approaching the flower covered fence. He sprang to his feet calling, "Ziva, they are here. My brother has arrived!"

Ziva rushed to the courtyard and hugged Muriel and Joanna. She then kissed Barak on both cheeks.

Nicky barely escaped her embrace.

"What a fine family. Come, come, I know you are tired from the long trip. We have long anticipated your visit. News of the events of the last month has reached us." She pushed a hand through her hair. "It is so good to see you here. Please plan to stay a long, long time."

Zedekiah's large frame moved quickly, as he grinned broadly. "Welcome, and I see you even brought the little donkey I left with you. You have never visited Caesarea before and I have much to show you. Tomorrow you get the grand tour."

*   *   *

The blue water lapped at the great stone walls around the harbor. The city was all new and the dressed stones of the tall buildings lined the straight streets. Hardly a cloud was visible. Zedekiah spread his arms. "This is the great port that has brought ships from all the world to our nation and, I might add, given us our prosperity."

Joanna muttered under her breath, "And all the wretched Romans."

Nicky squinted into the distance. "And when, Uncle, do we get to swim?"

"Ah, patience my nephew. I promise you, in two days we will all go to the sandy beach, and Ziva will fix a lunch fit for royalty. Today we see the marvels of our great city. A city where, once, only the lonely tower of Strato stood. Now thanks to old King Herod we have one of the finest ports in the Roman world. Caesarea is a center for the ships of the world."

Barak held Muriel's arm. "Isn't this splendid?"

She gazed at the horizon, her face blank.

They viewed the great curved amphitheater, seating over a thousand. The smooth seating polished bright, looked down on a stage that would hold a hundred actors. The Roman temple had six tall columns that were fluted and decorated with designs at the tops. Two lions flanked the steps leading to the entrance. The whole city and harbor was surrounded by massive walls and on the land side a moat. After a lunch in a little café, they visited the harbor filled with ships of many nations.

Nicodemus started toward the Roman trireme that rocked gently at the end of the long stone pier. The warship had a high ram on the front and long oars protruded from its double rows of ports. Guards stood at both ends of the war-ship. Nicky took one step toward the ship and Zedekiah gripped his shoulder, shaking his head.

Nearing the end of the day, Zedekiah led them down the main thoroughfare leading past a series of statues, the first of Caesar Augustus.

Zedekiah said nothing, but Joanna moaned. "They bring images of their gods here to defile our land."

Passing a Greek statue of a discus thrower, Nicky asked, "Don't they wear clothes?"

Zedekiah grinned. "The Greek word for the place of contest is 'gymnos'. That means to exercise in the nude." He mischievously glanced at the women. "Of course, no females are allowed. At least—"

Ziva poked him. "Zedekiah!"

Zedekiah hailed a passing citizen. "Ah, Marcos, allow me to introduce my brother from Jerusalem, a member of the Sanhedrin." He put his arm around Barak's shoulder. "And this man, my brother, is a Roman citizen who helped us build our synagogue."

Barak's face registered surprise. "You attend the synagogue?"

The Roman extended his arm, his handshake warm. "I'm not a proselyte ... at least not yet ... but yes, I often attend. I find the teachings of your God enlightening. I am happy to meet you, sir."

As Marcos headed off into the crowd, Joanna blurted, "You allow Romans in the synagogue?"

Zedekiah looked intently into her brown eyes. "Only the sons of Israel are in the inner chamber, but in the surrounding court of women, we have many God fearing people who come to worship. On this Sabbath you will be our honored guests. You will be impressed by our spacious new synagogue."

Nicky looked at his father, who merely spread his palms upward, and shrugged.

On the Sabbath, Nicodemus was surprised at the large number attending service and the openness of the partition between the men's inner court and the women's section. High on the eastern side of the high ceiling were pieces of blue, red and green glass that fractured the light flooding across the main rostrum. The raised platform was of dark, polished wood. The ark holding the Torah was ornately carved. He was also impressed by the number of non-Jewish men and women who sat behind the barrier. Barak was introduced by his brother and asked to give the admonition of the service. Nicodemus was given the honor of reading the text of the day. The cantor, a very excellent singer, led the congregation in a number of Psalms, and some songs Nicky had never heard before. It was a long service and he stole glances at the section behind the partition. The outsiders participated, particularly in the singing.

Walking from the service, Joanna strode beside Barak. "Father, I am sure I saw one of those who was with the soldiers who killed little Jessie. He was the one with the big nose. He may have even recognized us."

Barak put his finger to his lips. "I saw him too. I just don't know. Don't mention it to your mother."

"I wish I would have had a knife."

Barak wheeled to face her, his face red. "Would you then kill him ... in the meeting place of your God?"

Nicodemus watched as his sister and father stood in silence, glaring. They were an arm-span from each other and a world apart.

That evening, Ziva and Muriel were standing at the table peeling vegetables. The conversation was one-sided with Muriel merely nodding her head from time to time.

Finally, Ziva stabbed a cucumber and turned to her sister-in-law. "Muriel, I am sorry at the loss of little Jessie but ..."she turned, hands on hips. "Your two other children need a mother, and your daughter doesn't need more reason to justify her hatred." She frowned. "And your husband needs a wife."

Muriel's mouth dropped open, but Ziva continued. "I never thought my favorite sister-in-law would be wallowing in self pity."

Muriel slashed at her cucumber but said nothing.

*   *   *

Uncle Zedekiah, along with Barak's family, climbed the first ascent on the slope to Mount Carmel. Muriel, wearing a blue shawl, had her hair tied with a bright ribbon. She strode beside the little donkey who was more interested in the foliage surrounding the trail than the scenery.

Barak turned to Muriel. "It's getting steeper, if you'd like to ride for a while."

She lifted her head, a hint of a smile on her face. "I'm fine, it's a beautiful day."

The oak and pine trees surrounding the winding trail were fully clothed in green and contrasted with the blue ocean stretching toward the western horizon. Scattered red poppies bloomed everywhere and blue lupin cast a slight scent in the air.

Nicky pointed to the structure bordering the ocean. "Look Father, the aqueduct leads all the way back to where we swam yesterday."

Barak took a deep breath. "Yes, old Herod built that aqueduct well. Without it Caesarea could not exist. Do you realize it is the only decent port in all our land? Joppa is not deep enough to handle large ships." He pulled the donkey's rope. "You did well learning to swim yesterday."

"I almost swallowed the whole ocean. Father, where did you learn to swim so well? You even swim better than Uncle Zedekiah. He mainly floats." Then he glanced back at his uncle puffing up the hill.

Barak laughed. "But with his size, he floats well. Son, when I was a student, our family was poor and our families could not send us to the yeshiva you attend. We were sent to Capernaum on the Sea of Galilee. In the afternoons we spent much time swimming in the blue lake."

"Galilee, that's the sea of Tiberius, correct?"

"Yes, but for the Jews it will always be Galilee. It's beautiful, deep blue. Excellent fish come from there. The water is not like the ocean. You can even drink it. Across the lake you can see the hills of Gadara. It's as beautiful as this scene today."

"Someday, Father, I will go there."

The path had grown steep and the oak trees had given way to spruce. Myrtle wood and blooming plants overhung the trail. Finally they reached the crest and paused, waiting on Zedekiah.

Ahead was a clearing, in the center a clutter of rocks. Blue and purple anemones dotted the grass before them. Joanna sprinted to one patch of tiny white anise and plopped down. The rest of the family joined her. From this raised spot they viewed the coast line to the south and Caesarea in the distance.

Barak tied the donkey to a small shrub and unloaded the wicker basket and blankets. He stood gazing to the west where the mountain rose sharply before it dropped into the sea. He beckoned to Nicodemus. "This is probably the spot where the prophet Elijah faced the four hundred prophets of Baal." His hands reached wide. "This was the place where two altars were built, one to Jehovah and the other to the false god Baal." Pacing he continued. "Son, can you imagine? All the long day Priests of Baal implored and screamed for their God to answer by fire and take their sacrifice ..."

Nicky said softly, "But Baal didn't answer."

Barak looked approvingly. "No, as much as they cut themselves and cried out, Baal didn't answer." With palm uplifted, he continued. "At the time of the evening oblation, the prophet commanded his sacrifice to be placed on the altar to Jehovah ... then, Nicodemus, do you remember?"

Nicodemus stood. "Then he commanded his servants to douse the sacrifice and wood with water—three times—and then he prayed to God."

Barak's arm went around his son, his other lifted to heaven. His voice echoed across the meadow. "And then our God sent fire, blazing fire from heaven. Fire so intense the sacrifice, the wood, even the water was consumed." He squeezed his son. "Then the idolatrous priests were slaughtered." He paused, pointing to the surrounding field. "Right in this very place, our God answered with fire."

Joanna stood beside her father. "So our God does strike with vengeance?"

Barak paused, his face solemn. "Yes, my daughter, our God does strike the wicked, but he also can look into the hearts of all men."

Nicodemus pleaded, "Can you tell us the rest of the story, Father?"

Zedekiah exclaimed, "That, my boy, will be after we eat."

Barak clapped his hands. "Yes, now we eat."

After lunch Barak suggested, "The rest of our story could be better told from the summit of the mountain."

Both children were eager to lead the way and Muriel insisted on joining the family. Zedekiah, who had been snoring, stretched and yawned. "Me too, I guess." They ascended the steep incline.

From the top of Carmel, to the north they could see Ptolemais, and in the distance, Tyre. Tiny ships dotted the blue ocean. To the south they could even see the hills bordering the Valley of Sharon.

They perched on rocks around the summit and Barak began. "This mountain probably looked very different that year; it was three years of the worst drought in the history of Israel. Samaria too was parched, nothing grew."

He turned to Joanna. "Do you remember the story, my daughter?"

Joanna stood beside her father. "God had sent a drought to punish the nation for their sins. For three years not a drop fell on the land. Jezebel had sent her priests to stand against Elijah to prove her gods were right. After the slaughter of the false priests, it was then that Jehovah sent the rain."

Barak continued. "Elijah probably stayed below in our meadow, one which was covered with bodies of the false prophets. He commanded his servant to come up here and look toward the west, out over the ocean." Barak pointed to the horizon. "It was evening, the sky was as clear as it is now. The servant reported back to Elijah. Not even a small cloud was in sight."

He held out his hand to Nicodemus and his son picked up the narrative.

"And the prophet sent him here seven times. Then on the seventh time ..." He rose to stand beside his father and sister. " ...on the seventh time he saw a cloud, as small as a man's hand, rising from the ocean."

Barak smiled broadly as Nicodemus continued, "And Elijah told King Ahab to get to his chariot because Jehovah was about to violently end the drought."

Zedekiah joined his brother, his face solemn. "And it poured rain in such torrents the chariots got stuck in the mud."

Nicodemus stared at the ocean. "This is the spot where God spoke by sending his rain on a thirsty land."

Barak added, "By fire as well as by water. That was long ago in our past." He turned and looked at the little donkey grazing in the meadow below.

Nicodemus pointed to the animal. "Father, the owner of the donkey—and the baby—do you think God is speaking now? Perhaps in this time?"

Chapter Eight

Passover

TWELVE YEARS LATER

Nicodemus bounded up the steps two at a time, perhaps inappropriate for one in priestly robes. At twenty-five, he relished his jobs in the temple courts. He adjusted his yarmulke and brushed his blue embroidered cuff. It was difficult to move with dignity among all the people pressing toward the altar to present sacrifices. Many were visiting the temple for the first time. The sun was just peeking above the gates and it was encouraging to see such large crowds this early, but Passovers were always this way.

He hesitated, watching a boy standing between some older men. His uncles, dressed in formal attire, stood in a small huddle around the lad. The boy held the Torah as he chanted, his voice fluctuating between childhood and manhood.

Nicodemus' mind flashed back to twelve years before. Then, he too had stood to read the Torah in front of the great altar, the sun's rays flashing from the golden face of the temple. Back then, this scene was new and exciting. The excitement was still there, but his knowledge of the temple courts, hallways and rituals had become as familiar as the hills of Bethlehem. He chuckled as the young reader stumbled and the man to his side picked up the chant.

Memories were pushed aside as the crowd swirled around him. This was the great feast time. He shook his head. His nation needed a time of joy. There had been enough trouble in these past few years. Now, as a novice to the council, his role was to make sure the celebration reached a happy conclusion.

He saw Rabbi Samuel pushing through the throng toward him. "Ah, my good Nicodemus, it is good that you are early. It is a day when Israel rejoices. Sabbath in this city is so busy even the restrictions the Romans place on us don't stop our celebrating. We have had great crowds. It is sad that many on the hillsides are already folding their tents to return home. I have never seen the Hinnom Valley so full of sheep, and the hills around the walls must have had a thousand tents." The old teacher grinned, showing his missing tooth.

"Teacher, did you have a special reason for seeking me?"

Rabbi Samuel, eyes twinkling, exclaimed, "Last night my wife and I took a young man into our home. He spent Friday with the teachers in our inner court. He is from Nazareth. He reminds me of you when you first joined our yeshiva. He asks questions that surprise even Gamaliel. He knows the law very well for one so young."

"How old is he?"

"He's only twelve, the same age you were when we first met. He will be a guest of the scribes and teachers later this morning. If you can free yourself of the many chores of this day, come and I will introduce you. He is one who is beyond his years in understanding."

Nicodemus cocked his head. "Honored teacher, I will try to come, but my tasks for this day may prevent it. I thank you for the invitation."

It was afternoon before Nicodemus freed himself of his Sanhedrin duties and remembered Rabbi Samuel's invitation. Walking through the lower court he was surprised at the number of council members and priests he saw crowding Solomon's Colonnade. He twisted through the crowd and saw a young man seated among the scholars.

Gamaliel stood facing the youngster, his hand on his chin, listening.

The lad was of average height and had the wide shoulders and arms of one who knew heavy work. He wore a simple robe and well-worn sandals.

Nicodemus pushed closer to hear the boy speak. "My question is, Teacher, how do we understand the Sabbath restrictions, when David, a man of God's own heart, violated them?"

Nicodemus watched Gamaliel. The teacher, finger pointing heavenward, spoke. "You are correct young man. Often our restrictions and interpretations of God's law go against the intent of God's own heart. Your question is one that strikes the center of our practices."

The boy looked at Gamaliel, his forehead wrinkled. "Then rabbi, whose examples should we follow?" The young man looked at the faces around him, his eyes intense.

Just then, a tall man pushed his way forward, exclaiming to the boy, "Jesus, where have you been? Your mother and I have been looking all over the city for you? We were a day's journey toward Nazareth when we found you were not with our kinfolk."

A woman rushed to the boy and hugged him. After the embrace, she held him at arms-length and scolded. "Young man, why have you done this to us? Your father and I have been half out of our minds looking for you."

The boy, amazement on his face, looked at his mother. "Didn't you know I had to be in my Father's house?"

Looks were exchanged among the teachers, and Gamaliel placed his finger to his lips. Nicodemus felt a chill at the boy's answer. So his name was Jesus, named after their great leader Joshua; the one who had led the nation of Israel in the conquest of this land. What did this boy mean 'be in his Father's house'? His name was Jesus, but Nicodemus knew many with that name.

Nicodemus stared after the boy as he watched his parents lead him through the throng. Memories flooded his mind. Where had seen those people before?

Nicodemus saw his Uncle Joram seated among the scribes, still discussing their unusual guest. Joram stood and beckoned to his nephew. "I see you got to hear the boy. His questions reached into the heart of our understandings."

Joram stood and stretched. "Oh, by the way, did you hear my son Joseph is back from his studies in Rome? Because of stormy seas he missed the Passover meal, but he came in early this morning. We will be at your house tonight for a homecoming celebration. He is eager to see you. He is much changed. These years in Rome have made a big difference ... but, of course you will see. He even found a Jewish girl in Rome."

Nicodemus grinned. "Is the young woman—his discovery—going to be there?"

"No, we haven't met her yet. Her parents are strict Jewish people. She is still in Rome. She will be presented to us in good time. We will meet before sunset. Muriel is preparing a big feast."

* * *

Joseph had changed. His skin was tanned, his clothing more Roman, his face completely shaved. He smiled easily and stood very straight.

He greeted Nicodemus with a hug and a kiss on both cheeks, then hugged him again. "I have missed you, Nicky. In the five years in Rome, I often remembered our times together. Someday, you and I must visit the great city of Rome. It's splendid. Every hill has either a temple or magnificent government building."

Nicodemus punched his cousin playfully. "Yes, and I hear you've found a woman to your liking."

"Ah, my father's been talking, but yes, someday you will meet her. Her name is Rachel, she sings like a lark, and her eyes ... oh, her eyes, they are deep blue"

Nicodemus tilted his head. "Did she encourage you to shave, too?"

"No, all students of the forum are shaven. However, she was a little shocked when I did. As a matter of fact, she gave me a lecture about becoming too Roman. Her father is quite sick and she needs to care for him. But, perhaps when he gets better, she will come to visit us."

"I like her already. Now, you're back, are you going to apprentice to the Council?"

Joseph's brow wrinkled. "Cousin, my father and I have been considering. I am not sure whether I will be a member of the Sanhedrin. I can speak both the language of the Romans and Greeks. A position with the governor either here, or in Caesarea, is waiting for me. Or, if I decided, I could take over father's olive trade. The business has grown greatly. We now supply this city and are shipping our olive oil to many ports."

Nicodemus felt a surge of regret. "I was hoping that perhaps you'd come with me to the Galilee this summer. The Sanhedrin wants me to survey those cities in the north, and I also will be an apprentice teacher in Capernaum."

Joseph took Nicodemus' shoulders. "Cousin, I will try to visit you in the Galilee. I do remember our agreement to go to Galilee together." He gripped him firmly. "That was a long time ago. Many years have flown."

"Joseph, it's good to see you ... the new you. But don't you think we need someone on the council who knows the ways of Rome? We badly need one that speaks the language of both the Greeks and Romans. We have only one member who knows both those languages, and he is quite young. Your value to the Sanhedrin would be great. Besides our fathers are both leaders. Now, with Caiaphas engaged to the high priest's daughter, the Sadducees are a majority." He grinned. "Besides, we could spend the summer in Galilee. We had always promised to swim in that lake together.

Joseph bit his lip, his eyes boring into his cousin. "I will consider it carefully." A broad smile spread across his face. "Perhaps a trip to Galilee would be pleasant."

The crowds in the streets were thinning as Nicodemus made his way to the market. Muriel seemed to adapt to their new home in the busy city, even though she let her son do the market shopping. Today he had a long list of items. He made his way down the side streets to the stalls.

He was looking for the seller called Cloe. She was still as friendly as ever and just as big a flirt. He turned toward her tables of fruit, now thoroughly picked-over. He spotted her in the corner, and at first didn't recognize her or the man facing her. As the tall man turned the decoration on his flowing robe stood out and his curly hair identified him; it was Caiaphas, a fellow intern to the Council.

Nicodemus watched their conversation and saw Caiaphas put several coins in her hand. His hand slid from her shoulder down across her dress. Nicodemus stood frozen as Cloe reached up and kissed Caiaphas' cheek, grabbed his arm, and pulled him toward the alleyway behind the stand.

Nicodemus' stomach felt like someone had punched it—very hard.

*   *   *

Nicodemus looked out across the deep blue of the Sea of Galilee and watched the two young men splashing toward him. Both of the sons of Zebedee shook the water from their hair.

James chided, "Come on, teacher, you'll never learn to swim just staring at the water."

Nicodemus knew delaying would really tempt them to throw him in, so he jumped, clumsily hitting the clear, cold water. The shock quickly subsided and he tried his best to coordinate his strokes and breathing. By the end of the morning, he was getting it right, though he never managed the ease with which these sons of Zebedee moved through the water.

Drying on the beach, John scooted beside him. "Teacher, in our last session you said, 'We must forgive our enemies.' I find that very difficult."

Nicodemus shook the water from his beard while he considered his answer.

James joined them.

"John, I understand what you ask. There is much hatred in our world. Today, forgiveness is the opposite of most teaching. Tomorrow in class, we will discuss it." His finger tip touched his forehead, and he caught himself imitating his father's action. "Think about it, and on the morrow you will open our class."

"Will your cousin Joseph be there?"

"No, he has returned to Arimathea. His father required his help; it is near the time of preparation of their olive oil. Why do you ask?"

James punched his brother's arm. "He just thinks Joseph is not so strict with his evaluations."

Nicodemus caught himself being pleased at the comment. Perhaps his training under Gamaliel was taking hold.

Zebedee approached and gave a slight bow. "Ah, Teacher, I am glad you are enjoying our beautiful lake. I am pleased that one from the Council spends time with our young men." He turned to his sons. "Boys, there is much work to be done. We have fish to clean and nets to mend. Get your garments and I will meet you at the boat."

The boys rose and followed their father down the beach. Nicodemus watched another boat approaching the shore and he waved to the sons of Jonah as they beached their boat. "Good morning, Peter, Andrew. You must have had lots of fish to keep you on the lake after sunrise."

Peter, the taller of the two, jumped ashore and with a powerful lift, pulled the craft onto the beach. He muttered, "Lousy fishing all night, and we caught nothing."

That evening, as Nicodemus was dining with Simon, a fellow Pharisee, he commented on their fine synagogue. "It is good our fellow Jews are so aware of a need for an adequate place to meet. Your synagogue here in Capernaum is well-appointed."

Simon chuckled. "My young friend, the Jews of Capernaum are as tight as misers. Most of our new building was paid for by a Roman centurion."

Nicodemus took a deep breath. "A Roman, and a centurion? This is indeed a surprise."

Simon shook his knife. "If more Romans were like this man, we'd have a lot fewer Zealots trying to kill them. Here in this city, thanks to this man, there is peace."

* * *

As summer drew to a close, Nicodemus returned to Jerusalem. He headed down the Jordan Valley, still lush with grass, and followed the well-worn path toward the Dead Sea. Descending the valley, the land became dry and the temperature soared. By the time Jericho came in sight, he was sweating heavily, his cloak relegated to the bundle on his back. Ahead, he saw the palm trees swaying in the slight breeze. They edged the fortress built by Herod. The vapor from the Dead Sea was rising in the distance. He looked to the west and wondered which of the great buildings imprisoned his father and the other leaders during those last days of Herod's life. On the outskirts of the old city, he stopped to refresh himself at the crowded spring. The remains of the wall that had fallen fifteen hundred years before were still visible. He tried to visualize that army of Joshua silently marching around the city. He almost imagined the fear of those inside the walls when the trumpets and shouting violently ended the strange siege. How did those people feel as their defending walls collapsed around them and they faced the desert-hardened army of Joshua?

He watched the people drawing the water from the spring and wondered if they were really aware of the history of this place. He caught himself guessing what Joshua might say to see his people enslaved. How would he have reacted to a half-breed king like Herod building a fortress just a bow shot from the spot where God had destroyed the first Jericho? He shook his head—the Jews needed a Joshua today, a deliverer.

Chapter Nine

Joanna

SIXTEEN YEARS LATER

Nicodemus strode across the temple court toward the Beautiful Gate. He glanced up at the eagle claw, the only remains of the bronze eagle Herod placed there. Had it really been thirty years since the young men had hacked it from its perch and burned to death for their deed of rebellion? Now, with Herod's son Archelaus dead and his rein of terror over, Nicodemus, like all the Jews, hoped for a peaceful time under the new Roman legate, Pontius Pilate. Only time would tell, but Roman soldiers still roamed the streets, their short swords ready.

He pushed through the market, barely glancing at Cloe. She now wore heavy face paint and flashing earrings. Time had changed her from a beautiful girl into a used woman in these short years. He picked a few vegetables from a nearby vendor and hurried home. He hung his outer robe on a peg.

Muriel looked up from her mending. "Ah, my son, you look tired today." She poured him a glass of water. "Perhaps, soon my son you will consider finding a good Jewish girl to greet you when you come home. I was talking to the Rabbi Samuel. You know, son, his granddaughter is—"

"Mother, just because Joseph found a wife doesn't mean I am ready to marry. When time comes ..."

His mother turned away, shrugging her shoulders. "You are over forty now ... I had hoped. Now with Barak gone—may God rest his soul ..." She picked up her sewing basket and sighed.

That evening, there was a rap on the door. When Muriel answered it, she threw her arms wide. "My daughter! Oh, Joanna, it is good to see you!" She embraced her and stroked the gray hairs in her daughter's temple. "You don't have to knock to enter this house. It has been too long, come in, come in."

"Thank you, Mother," Joanna collapsed into a chair. Nicodemus moved a chair to face her. He took her shoulders. "Joanna, it's been so long since you've been home. Please stay as long as you can." He felt her hands, noticing how rough they had become, wrinkles etching the brown skin. "We heard you and Nathan were on the Jordan."

Joanna bit her lip. "Nathan is dead!" Her jaw clenched. "Two years ago."

Her shoulders pulsed, finally she wiped her nose.

Muriel stroked her hair. "We didn't know ... We didn't know. What happened?"

Joanna sniffed, took a deep breath, her jaw rigid. "They murdered him. Those cruel men murdered him." Her chin quivered. "They hung him on a cross. They crucified him, Nathan ... with nine others. It was just outside Jericho. Archelaus ordered death for all the Zealots he captured." She took a deep breath and turned to Nicodemus. "It was two years ago when Nathan was arrested and crucified. Someone killed a Roman, and an order went out from Archelaus to kill ten Jews for the crime. Nathan and his friends weren't involved. I think the soldiers really knew it wasn't them, but those were the orders." She straightened. "They suffered horribly. One of our young men asked a guard if we could end their torture, and the Roman guard allowed him to break all of the men's legs."

Muriel blurted, "Soldiers broke their legs?"

Joanna shook her head. "No Mother, our fellow Zealot did that to stop the suffering."

Muriel's brow wrinkled. "I don't understand."

Nicodemus explained, "When the legs are broken, then the prisoner cannot force his body upward to breathe. He suffocates quickly. They broke their legs to hasten death."

He studied his sister. "You didn't come home after that. Why? Archelaus died two years ago."

Joanna wiped her eyes. "I didn't know where to go. I found a band of men who followed one called John the Baptizer. He was preaching near Salem on the Jordan and great crowds came to be baptized. Even soldiers came to be baptized by him."

Nicodemus exclaimed, "Romans?"

She nodded. "Also, some Pharisees came from your Council to hear him. John chastised them strongly. He was really severe with them."

"Members of the Sanhedrin were there, on the Jordan?"

"He told them to repent, and bring forth deeds worthy of repentance. Most of them left angry. I began to listen to his teachings and it changed my life. I went to work in a vineyard for one of John's followers, but just last week, soldiers came from Herod the Tetrarch. They arrested John and bound him. The crowd almost rioted, but John calmed them, and submitted to the soldiers. With his arrest, our band dissolved. That's the reason I came here. May I stay and rest?" Her eyes searched their faces. "So much has changed."

"The Baptizer is in prison? Where?"

"I don't know. But he's not a Zealot, he was just teaching us to do right things."

Nicodemus stared at his sister. "Are you still a Zealot?"

Joanna's words were halting. "I'm tired of hating. John taught us not to hate. John also spoke of one who is coming, the Messiah. John said he was unworthy to even untie this messiah's sandals.

Nicodemus shuddered. Just yesterday rumors had reached the Sanhedrin. One claiming to be the Messiah was stirring the nation in the region of the Galilee.

*　*　*

The morning sun was warming the air as Nicodemus crossed the temple pavement. He joined Gamaliel and they strolled together toward the great white building.

Gamaliel spoke softly. "I have known you for many years, and now you are a full member of the Council. We need to discuss a mission I'd like you to undertake. It's for those of us who still uphold the Holy Word." He paused and lifted his finger. "Come to my home this evening. You will eat with us, and I will tell you more of my plans then."

That evening Nicodemus wound his way to the bigger homes in the Holy City. He felt intimidated by Gamaliel's invitation. Before he rapped on the door, he adjusted his robe and smoothed his beard. A young woman answered and invited him in. The large home in the old section was carpeted, tapestries covering two walls. On one other wall, codex and scrolls were stacked in shelves reaching to the ceiling.

Gamaliel greeted him and ushered him into an enclosed courtyard where a table was set with blue dishes. He motioned toward the young woman. "This is the last of my daughters, Deborah. She, along with my wife and I, occupies this large place. All of my other children have chosen to live away from me, and I only see my grandchildren on feast days."

Deborah tilted her head. "We will serve you soon. Mother is finishing the preparation."

Nicodemus watched Deborah as she moved quickly toward the adjoining room. "Your daughter is attractive," he whispered.

Gamaliel slapped his fist into his hand. "Not attractive enough to find a husband, or perhaps, it is that she is too much like her namesake."

"You mean the Deborah who judged Israel and led the battle on Mount Tabor?"

"Yes, and I'm also afraid my daughter is also too much like her father. I have always spoken in judgment when perhaps I should have remained quiet. She often achieves the same effects with her words."

Gamaliel walked to the door and closed it carefully. "Let me tell you the reason that I wanted to talk to you. Annas has sent two of the older members of the Sanhedrin north into Galilee to investigate the growing restlessness around this Jesus of Nazareth. Those people are saying he is the long-awaited Messiah. Ahaz and Bava, are going there and I am not confident in their—shall I say—openness? Their minds seem to be closed to anything different."

Nicodemus blinked. The reason for his invitation hit him. "And since I have been there, you are thinking ...?"

"Correct, you are a good one to look at the facts and bring back information that will be balanced and fair."

Just then, the women entered, bringing plates of food, and Nicodemus watched Deborah. She was not only graceful, but her dark eyes fascinated him. Their eyes met. He was the first to glance away, his face flushed.

After dinner, Deborah ushered him out. "I have heard many good things of you from my father. We need to become better acquainted." A trace of a smile flickered across her face.

He felt foolish as he stood speechless at her bold invitation.

She closed the door.

Chapter Ten

Galilee

Nicodemus splashed ashore. Today, his swim far out into Lake Galilee was exhilarating. He looked at the snowy top of Mt. Hermon to the north. It was a glorious sunny morning. He dried himself with the towel and remembered his first attempts at swimming here years ago when he and Joseph were teachers of the Capernaum yeshiva.

He gingerly stepped across the rough stones to a bench where he slipped into his robe and sandals. He straightened the sleeves so the ornate designs along the cuffs were visible. Now, as a full-fledged member of the Sanhedrin, he wore the emblems with pride.

He waved to Zebedee who was mending nets while perched on the edge of his boat.

Zebedee stretched. "I used to swim like that ... a long time ago. I see your feet are not toughened yet. I don't even feel the rocks with my bare feet."

Nicodemus walked over to the boat. "Where are your sons?"

Zebedee tossed his net aside. "James and John, along with the sons of Jonah, have gone with the Nazarene off into the hills to the north."

"Andrew and Peter, they have become disciples of the Nazarene?"

"Ever since they went to the Jordan with the Baptizer—that's where they met this Jesus—they are different." He put a rope inside the boat. "He appointed a few men to be his apostles."

"Apostles? How long ago did this happen?"

"About three weeks past. This Nazarene said he was going to make them fish for men. Since then, both Jonah and I have had to fish alone without sons to help."

Nicodemus studied the weathered face. "Are you two men going to be able to earn enough without your sons? John was telling me how hard it was to catch enough fish."

Zebedee chuckled. "Just before they left to go with Jesus they caught more fish at one time than we usually catch in a month. In fact, it took Jonah and me a whole day to clean them. The boys had fished all night and caught nothing. Then, just as they were giving up, the Nazarene appeared and told them to cast their net on the other side. I still can't figure how they caught all those big ones and didn't tear the nets. Anyway, we sold that load of fish for two months' wages for both of us."

"The Nazarene even does his tricks with fish?"

"Can't say it was a trick. I've fished this lake all my life and I've never seen such a catch." He pointed north. "They've headed into the hills of Caesarea Philippi just yesterday."

"On the slopes of Mount Hermon?"

"I think that's where they went." He dropped his awl. "You hear what happened in our synagogue last week? The ruler, Jairus ... his daughter was raised from the dead by the Nazarene."

"What do you mean 'raised from the dead?'"

"The girl, Jairus' only daughter, died five days ago."

"She died? I'm sure his family must be devastated."

"You don't understand. She isn't dead ... not anymore."

"Not dead? What are you saying?" Nicodemus grasped the fisherman's shoulders.

Zebedee moved his face close. "That's what I am saying. The one from Nazareth—this Jesus—he passed through our town several days ago. The mourners were all assembled. Then, this healer came and went inside the house. Next thing we knew he came out and the girl was beside him."

"This healer from Nazareth was here, in Capernaum? And I just missed him."

"When he was here two weeks ago he was in the synagogue and he cast out an evil spirit, one that had tormented a man for years. That man's no longer a lunatic." Zebedee scratched his cheek. "Strange things have happened in our city these last few weeks."

"Will the Nazarene come back here?"

"No telling. He's always moving around. You see all these people in our town? Many have come to be healed by this teacher. My sons have been with him more than here with me. They listen to his every word. If you want to see him, he'll probably head to Jerusalem for the feast."

"Jesus will be at the Passover? Will you be there?"

Zebedee shook his head "Someone needs to catch the fish. I'd like to visit my brother who lives in the city. He's a steward to the high priest ... name is Malcus."

"Steward to Caiaphas?"

Zebedee spit on the ground. "No, not that strutting donkey, the real high priest, Annas." He looked sheepish. "Forgive me. I know I should not curse the high priest of my people, but ever since Caiaphas married into the priesthood ..." He cinched his belt. "Annas used to be a happy man, now ... my brother says it's just, just different."

Nicodemus shook his head. "Yes, I know Caiaphas well." He pointed to the crowd gathered in the road. "Zebedee, I need to talk to the synagogue ruler. Tell the boys hello when they return." He shook his head in disgust. "And I just missed the Nazarene."

He walked to the marketplace adjacent to the synagogue. Thoughts were tumbling through his mind like a waterfall. The Sanhedrin had sent him here to investigate rumors, but one raised from the dead? How could this be anything but the hand of God? —That is, if it were true.

He knocked at the door of the house adjoining the synagogue, the home of Jairus. A girl, about ten years old, with twinkling eyes answered the door. Nicodemus started to speak, but his words froze as he stared at the girl, Jairus only had one daughter.

Jairus greeted him and kissed his cheeks. "Come in, Teacher. This is a happy time in our home. Come in."

It was two hours later when Nicodemus left Jairus' home.

There was no doubt in the family's mind about the miracle. They had even begun to prepare her body for burial when Jesus appeared. Jairus explained that Peter and the sons of Zebedee had also witnessed the healing.

Nicodemus hurried to the home where the other Sanhedrin members were staying. Bava had already returned to Jerusalem. Only Ahaz was there. Ahaz stopped writing and looked up. Nicodemus suppressed a grin.

Ahaz's portly figure spilled over both sides of the small chair. "Well my young colleague, I am preparing my report. Perhaps I should include some of your observations. This assumed miracle of the daughter of Jairus has to be mentioned ...discreetly, of course.

I'm sure the 'miracle' was just some mistake, even though I was not here when it occurred. Probably the little girl had only seemed to have died. No creditable person testified of it." He blotted the ink on his paper. "I met this Jesus several weeks ago. He was clearly in violation of the Sabbath."

"How did he violate the Sabbath?"

"This Nazarene rigged a fake healing of a possessed man on the Sabbath—in the synagogue! When I reprimanded him on his violation of the Sabbath, he called me a hypocrite. It was not a pleasant encounter."

"And did you investigate the possessed man's history?"

"Well no, but it was obviously a trick."

"Did you talk to Jairus about his daughter?"

Ahaz reddened. "Young man, I was a member of the Council twenty years before you were admitted. Are you questioning my ability to discern?"

"Have you been to Nazareth?" Nicodemus knew full well his portly associate would have avoided the steep climb to the city of Nazareth if at all possible.

Ahaz glared at him. "I will be leaving here tomorrow. When we get to Jerusalem, we should meet before we submit our report." With that, he returned to his writing.

Nicodemus knew Ahaz well, and what his report would say.

Ahaz rolled his letter. "Before I left the synagogue, I charged the congregation to beware of this false prophet."

That night Nicodemus sat, pen in hand, and wasted several sheets of papyrus trying to write his confusing thoughts. He stared at the lake. A star twinkling on the horizon reminded him of a scene so many years ago, when he was a boy on a roof in Bethlehem. That was thirty years ago. Now ... who was this one? This one from Nazareth ...

Could it be? He'd finish his report later. Tomorrow he had a mountain to climb.

*   *   *

It took three hours, all uphill to reach Nazareth. Sitting in the room of the synagogue ruler, he skipped the formalities and got quickly to his questions. "This Jesus grew up here?"

The old rabbi adjusted his yarmulke. "Yes, he was the son of Joseph the carpenter, along with his three brothers. His mother and sisters were also part of our synagogue for many years. After the death of Joseph, he left for some time and he returned less than a month ago. We had heard of his miracles, but when he came here he didn't do any great signs." He sipped his tea. "In fact, he enraged everyone so much the young men were going to throw him off the cliff outside town."

"They were going to throw the healer off a cliff? What happened?"

The old man spread his hands and shook his head. "That's the strange thing ..."

"Well?"

"Jesus ... just walked through the crowd."

"You mean he ran, and—"

The rabbi shook his head. "No, he just walked through the mob."

"This is his home town? So you knew him well?"

The synagogue ruler squirmed; "Just tell the Sanhedrin we weren't at all impressed by him. I can't say more."

That evening, Nicodemus finished his report. He poured candle wax on the edge and pressed his ring to it. Someday he had to see this healer. Then he remembered, perhaps he already had, years ago, in the temple.

* * *

Nicodemus knew that instead of descending the Jordan River to reach Jerusalem, often Jesus took the more direct route, through the land of the Samaritans. Like all Jews, Nicodemus had avoided taking that route on previous trips. It was one thing to take a shorter way, but quite another to stay with Samaritans. Perhaps, he thought, he could discover more by traveling that way to Jerusalem. He shuddered. No self-respecting Council member would dare eat or sleep in the land of the Samaritans.

The next day Nicodemus approached Sychar. Traveling along, he was aware of the stares of the Samaritans. He knew the hatred between his people and these half-breeds. He glanced at Mount Gerizim, just ahead. They claimed to follow the Jewish law, and then built their own temple on top of the mountain ahead. He'd heard about their pagan worship, but outside of their hostile stares, he had not encountered any trouble.

He reached the wall of Sychar as the sun was at midday. He was tempted to stop in the marketplace to find some food, but imagined the reaction of his fellow Council members if they heard of it.

He rested on the curbing of the city well. He knew of this well; it was one dug by their ancestor Jacob, two-thousand years before.

A young man had just finished drawing water and stared at him. Setting his jar down, he spoke softly. "You want water?"

Obviously the boy did not understand the animosity between their nations. Nicodemus replied gently, "Yes, I would like some water."

The boy sloshed some into a cup and passed it to Nicodemus. "My mother says, now, we even give water to Jews."

Nicodemus leaned toward the lad. "Your mother instructed you to give water to strangers?"

"Yes, even Jews." The boy's smile was warm.

Nicodemus almost laughed. "What made your mother say that, young man?" He tasted the cool water.

"Ever since that Nazarene came here, we're supposed to be nice to everyone."

Nicodemus' brows almost touched. "The Nazarene ... the one who heals ... was here in Samaria?"

The boy's head pumped up and down. "And he healed a whole bunch of people ... and my cousin who was blind ... she can see now, just as good as I."

"He was here, the healer was here?" He took a long drink. "How long ago?"

"Few weeks back. He stayed next door to our house. You want to talk to my mom about him? She spent a whole lot of time talking to him about stuff."

Nicodemus stood and handed the cup to the boy. Almost in a trance, he walked down the road. The healer had even stayed with the half-breed Samaritans ... and healed them. How could he report this to the Sanhedrin?

* * *

It was evening the next day when Nicodemus kicked off his sandals in Jerusalem. Muriel brought him a basin of water for his feet and a cup of warm broth.

Nicodemus stretched. "It's good to be home. This has been a long three weeks."

Muriel began cutting bread. "Now, with Barak gone, this house is lonely. I almost wish we were back in Bethlehem."

Nicodemus watched his mother as she bent to add wood to the brazier. Her hair was almost entirely white and her back bent. He too missed his father, now two years dead. If he were alive today, what would he tell the Council about this healer from Nazareth? Barak had eagerly looked for the Messiah. How would he react to this one, and what would his report say?

The following day, Nicodemus presented his parchment to Annas, the high priest. Instead, Caiaphas snatched it and broke the seal. He glanced at it, then tossed it on a stack of scrolls beside his chair. "Tuesday next, when we meet, we will review all of these. We would appreciate a verbal summation of your visit to the north. Ahaz and Bava have already given us much information." He yawned. "I suppose you might add something. Just don't take too much of the Council's time. We have much to discuss."

* * *

Tuesday, the full Council assembled. Nicodemus shortened what he planned to say as much as possible. The better part of the morning was spent with information on the growing unrest, not only in Galilee, but in Judea as well. Great crowds were following the Nazarene and reports of healings were everywhere.

Nicodemus was relieved that Joseph had again rejoined the Council. He and his cousin were both surprised that the Pharisees— those who believe in a miraculous God—seemed as alarmed by the reports as the more liberal Sadducees.

It was the afternoon session before Caiaphas stood and motioned to Nicodemus. "Nicodemus, who has just returned from the Galilee, has given me this report. Allow me to read this in part, since our time is fleeting." He opened the parchment and read from the last section, which did not include the raising of Jairus' daughter. He faced Nicodemus. "And so, the people of Nazareth had the foresight to expel this false prophet from their midst?" He leaned forward. "Is this correct?"

Nicodemus flushed and rose. "At Nazareth ... yes, but while in Capernaum—"

Caiaphas interrupted. "Let's focus on your Nazareth visit first."

Nicodemus stumbled through his summation, but when he tried to continue, Caiaphas cut him off. "As we meet in groups perhaps you might give a more complete summation. At this time, it is important that we hear from others." His smile was condescending. "We certainly don't want to prolong our session until midnight."

Nicodemus plopped to his seat and caught the eye of Gamaliel who was shaking his head, eyes cast down.

As the Council dismissed, several close members of the Council gathered around Nicodemus and Joseph. Rabbi Samuel placed his hand on Nicodemus. "There are whispers that the Teacher will be here in Jerusalem for the coming feast. That is only two weeks away. Perhaps—and this is just a thought—you should find where he will be staying. I understand he is a close friend of one Lazarus who lives in Bethany."

Chapter Eleven

Night

It was dark except for the moon as Nicodemus passed the ancient olives trees, their shadows throwing long fingers that danced in the gusting breeze. The lights of Bethany flickered at the crest of the hill. He asked himself for the twentieth time if he was really prepared for what lay ahead. What would the Council say if they knew of his visit? Secrets in this land rarely stayed hidden. What if he were seen? He slipped into the shadows as a throng of young men came down the path. They were laughing as they passed, and he wished his heart were that free. Reaching the town he glanced both ways, then softly approached. He repeated his sister's directions: two-story dwelling third from the end of the eastern street, an arched gateway.

He hesitated before he touched the door. He didn't know whether to wish the Nazarene was here or not. He tapped lightly, his heart thudding. A woman near his age opened the door after a second knock. Her eyes searched his.

"I come seeking Jesus. Is he here?"

The woman studied his face. "Why do you come?"

Nicodemus, realizing he didn't really know, blurted, "I wanted to meet the one they call the healer."

"Do you seek healing?" She stepped back and Nicodemus saw her face. She had a calm beauty. "Please come in. He is here. He's been very busy all day. He is resting, or perhaps praying. I'll call him." She motioned to a circle of chairs. A number of small oil lamps added a soft glow to the room. "Please sit down."

Nicodemus heard a quiet conversation in the adjoining room. His heart was still pounding. The woman pushed aside the drape. A slight smile crinkled her cheek. "He will see you. May I get you something to drink?"

Nicodemus had barely requested water when a tall figure entered the room. A tingle ran up his spine as he stared at the man walking to a chair facing him. The healer was simply dressed in a garment that hung to his bare feet. He had a slight beard, but it was his deep gray eyes that seemed to penetrate Nicodemus' very soul. The image of Jairus' daughter and her healing flashed through his mind.

Jesus sat studying Nicodemus, and then asked, "Why do you come, Nicodemus?"

Nicodemus recoiled. How did this one know his name? No one was to know of his mission. He tried to gather his thoughts and began his prepared words. "Rabbi, we know you are a teacher who has come from God. For no one could perform the miraculous signs you are doing if God were not with him."

The lamps illuminated the healer's face. His words were gentle. "I tell you the truth, no one can enter the kingdom of God unless he is born of water and the Spirit."

The words were not in any way what Nicodemus had anticipated. His mind spun. The Nazarene's response leaped ahead to the deep question of Nicodemus' own heart. He sat in stunned silence, and then blurted, "How can this be? Surely he cannot enter a second time into his mother's womb to be born!"

Jesus studied Nicodemus. "I tell you the truth, no one can enter the kingdom of God unless he is born of the water and the spirit. You should not be surprised at my saying.You must be born again. The wind blows wherever it pleases. You hear the sound, but you cannot tell where it comes from or where it is going. So it is with everyone born of the Spirit."

Nicodemus felt a chill at the chastisement.

Jesus' words, you must be born of the water and the spirit, sent more questions flooding through Nicodemus' mind. Why would he speak of the wind?

Nicodemus was hardly aware that his fingernails were biting into his palms. "How can this be?"

"You are Israel's teacher, and you don't understand? I tell you the truth, we speak of what we know, and we testify to what we have seen, but still you people do not accept our testimony."

Nicodemus felt Jesus' hand touch his.

"I have spoken to you of earthly things and you do not believe; how then will you believe if I speak of heavenly things?"

Nicodemus felt like he was a yeshiva student trying to remember his lessons.

Jesus looked deep into his eyes. "No one has ever gone into heaven except the one who came from heaven—the Son of Man. Just as Moses lifted up the snake in the desert, so the Son of Man must be lifted up, that everyone who believes in him may have eternal life.

Was Jesus calling himself the Son of Man? What was this lifting up?

Jesus sat back and after a moment smiled. "For God so loved the world that he gave his one and only Son, that whoever believes in him shall not perish but have eternal life."

Chills went up Nicodemus' spine as he looked into the teacher's face.

"For God did not send his Son into the world to condemn the world, but to save the world through him."

The teacher continued as Nicodemus listened. These were not the words of a promoter or false prophet. Nicodemus focused on every word, listening so intently he hardly was aware Jesus was touching his hand. When Jesus spoke of light coming into darkness and men loving darkness he caught himself nodding in agreement.

Their conversation lasted until the woman entered the room.

She spoke softly. "Forgive my interruption, but, it is late. Jesus, I know you must be very tired."

Jesus' eyes twinkled. He stood. "May I introduce Mary, sister of Lazarus and Martha." He turned to her. "Mary, this man is Nicodemus, one of the Sanhedrin. We will see him again." He rose and grasped Nicodemus' hand.

As Nicodemus walked down the hill, his head was spinning, but somehow his heart felt a hollow longing. Looking up at the white temple gleaming in the moonlight, he shuddered. He dreaded his thought of the coming meeting of the Sanhedrin, and their plans for this prophet of Nazareth, this gentle teacher.

When he reached the Kidron Brook, he gazed at the bright stars above. He lifted his eyes and started to pray. He was hardly aware he had dropped to his knees in the soft grass.

It was very late when he arrived home. Joanna rose from where she was mending. "You are very late, my brother." Her voice expressed mild concern. "May I warm some food for you?"

He shook his head. "Joanna, you've changed. This time away has made you a ... a different person. The hatred is gone. How did this happen?"

Joanna merely studied his robe. "My brother, it looks as though you have soiled your best robe. You've been on your knees." The expression on her face asked a thousand questions but she turned and moved the water kettle over the fire. "Take off the robe." There was silence as she worked, then she turned and tilted her head. "You've been to see Jesus, haven't you?"

Nicodemus had the robe halfway over his head when she asked. He froze. "How did you know?"

Joanna took the robe and examined the stain. She didn't speak until she had moved a basin and cleaning powder to the table. As the water heated, she turned. "You asked what changed me. I need to tell you the whole story. Nathan and I were hoping John the Baptizer would lead our rebellion, but he was a different kind of leader." She poured water into the basin and plunged the robe into it. "Instead of rebellion against the Romans, he taught us to change our way of thinking. Nathan became a different person because of John. I found myself letting go of my hatred. Then Jesus came to the Jordan."

"Jesus came to John the Baptizer?"

Joanna rubbed the cleansing powder into the garment and massaged the stains. "Nathan and I were both baptized just the day before the Nazarene came to be baptized himself." She plunged the garment into the pan and turned, her eyes searching her brother. "When John saw Jesus coming to be baptized he said, 'I should be baptized by you,' but Jesus told him he had come to complete all righteousness. When John plunged him into the water both Nathan and I saw something like a dove descending on Jesus."

Nicodemus looked up. "A dove?"

Joanna pushed the robe under the water. "I don't think it was a real dove, it seemed to be some sort of ... of ... like a vapor. When

Jesus came out of the water, John proclaimed, 'Behold, the Lamb of God that takes away the sins of the world.'"

Nicodemus pulled his undergarment tight. "Did the Nazarene stay there with John on the Jordan?"

"He left after a few days and many of John's disciples went with him. Nathan and I were married by John that week there on the Jordan." She glanced at him, her brown eyes troubled. "It was only three weeks later when the Roman soldier was murdered." She rubbed the robe vigorously.

"Is that when they killed Nathan and the others?"

Joanna froze, and then nodded. Examining the robe again, she squeezed it dry. Hanging it by the fire, she walked to her brother. "I know you have been troubled by the teachings of Jesus. I knew it would only take time before you met him. When you asked for directions to the home of Lazarus and his sisters, I knew. Sometimes, my brother, coming to belief is a matter as simple as washing dirt from a child's garment. At other times it is like getting rid of grass stains."

Nicodemus rubbed his hands together, his voice choked. "Why can't I believe in him? I have seen the little girl he raised from the dead. I have talked to a Samaritan boy that saw a blind girl healed. Tonight, when Jesus said I had to be born again I just couldn't ..." He dropped his head into his hands.

"Brother, I know how important your position on the Council is to you, but unless that becomes of less value than what you know is true ..."

Nicodemus' eyes were red as he faced Joanna. "My father was a member of the Council. My best friends are members. Gamaliel, the great teacher of the Law, is there. Am I to give all this up? For what? For someone who doesn't fit any of our concepts of a Messiah?"

Joanna dropped to her knees before her brother. "Do you remember when we were children ... that night of the shepherds? That baby wasn't born in a palace, but a cow barn. He didn't fit our father's expectations, did he?"

Nicodemus stood abruptly, his mind still whirling. "It's very late my sister. I need to sleep."

Chapter Twelve

Sanhedrin

The council chamber was packed. Nicodemus scooted close to Joseph and whispered, "It looks like everyone came to hear what's happening."

Joseph straightened his gown. "There is talk the Nazarene will be in the temple this feast day. My cousin, it seems even our fellow Pharisees are ready to challenge him."

Nicodemus wanted to share his encounter with Jesus the previous evening, but not here. He watched the high priests take their place. "Looks like Caiaphas is showing off a new robe. He reminds me of a peacock."

Annas, the former high priest, was seated beside Caiaphas. He raised his arms for silence. The members mumbled into stillness. "This day we are assembled to meet a growing threat to our God given place in our nation ..." He continued with a long opening statement, covering the reactions of the masses to the teaching of this Nazarene, Jesus. He ended his summation with a word of caution. "Remember, only last year our new regent, Pontius Pilate, mixed the blood of worshipers with their sacrifices. He is not timid. Also, let none of you think this false messiah is not intelligent. He has already, through his sly words, withstood some of our best minds. We must plan carefully our confrontations with this imposter. I will ask you to form small groups to devise questions to trap him in his speech. We cannot be embarrassed by him again."

Rabbi Samuel, seated behind Nicodemus, muttered, "Sounds as though the Sadducees have already made up their minds about this one."

Nicodemus' heart was burning to challenge Annas but he remained silent—again. Disgusted with himself, he castigated his timidity.

Annas dismissed the assembly into small units. Nicodemus, Joseph, and Gamaliel were the last to reach the private chamber reserved for the Pharisees. Nicodemus sighed as he watched Gamaliel lead the men in prayer. In spite of his gray hair, he was as imposing as ever. The small unit of twenty began work.

Ahaz rose. "I have been asked by Caiaphas to plan our questions for this deceitful false messiah. Do you have suggestions?"

Gamaliel stood. His voice held an edge. "It seems as though you men have already made an evaluation of this man's character. I would hope you have not judged too early." He turned and strode from the chamber.

Rabbi's Jason and Ahaz tried to restore order—everyone was talking at once. Joseph stood and gestured to Nicodemus. Without a word both followed Gamaliel from the chamber.

*   *   *

The following day, Nicodemus was in the upper room of Joseph's home. It faced the broad stairway leading to the temple platform. Both men watched the quadrangle of the lower level and the crowds pushing and crowding toward the Court of the Gentiles. As on most feast days, the sellers were manning their tables. The money changers were hawking their best deals. The bustle around the hastily constructed 'animals for sacrifice' pens, added to the clamor and smell.

Suddenly, shouting and confusion erupted. A shower of coins bounced down the stairway and cursing money changers rushed to retrieve them. Other dealers scurried down the stairs clutching bags of coins. Pigeons flooded the air and a flock of lambs poured down the stairway, their owners trying to stop their flying hoofs. A booming voice thundered, "My Father's house is a house of prayer and you have made it a den of robbers!"

Nicodemus jumped to his feet and pointed. "What's happening? Look, the temple guards are rushing in." He watched as priests, clutching their robes, followed the guards.

Within a minute, a tall figure holding a whip-like bundle of cords stood at the top of the staircase glaring at the merchants. His eyes were blazing as he ordered, "Get these animals and this filthy money out of here!"

Joseph exclaimed, "It's Jesus!"

Nicodemus was aghast. The man who had spoken to him so gently was commanding everyone with deadly authority. Even the guards stood frozen, not even attempting to stop him. One priest cried, "By what authority are you doing this?" Jesus turned. Nicodemus could only see his back, but the voice commanded, "This is the house of God! You have made it a den of robbers!"

Joseph chuckled. "Looks like the Nazarene's come to Jerusalem."

Within minutes the scene quieted. A crowd gathered on the staircase to listen to the teacher. Joseph poured a goblet of wine for his cousin and they sat looking down at Jesus and the people. They had a bird's-eye view of the scene. The crowds increased as Jesus spoke. At the top of the staircase a company of priests and scribes whispered among themselves.

Nicodemus observed, "Most of those following Jesus look like people from the countryside. He seems to attract more common folk."

The teacher, his hands outstretched to the crowd, spoke gently. "I say to you, beware the leaven of the scribes and Pharisees, they bind heavy burdens on men's shoulders, and do not lift a finger to help them."

Nicodemus punched his cousin. "I'll bet old Ahaz didn't like that."

Jesus, lifting his gaze to the crowd, commanded; "You shall love your neighbor as yourself."

One man, dressed in rich clothing, called out, "All the commands of Moses I have kept from my youth up. What must I do to inherit eternal life?"

Jesus fastened his eyes on the young man. "You know the commandments ..."

The young man replied, "I have kept them from childhood."

Jesus walked over and placed his hand on his shoulder. "Go, sell everything you have, and give it to the poor, then come and follow me."

The young man's face turned pale. He rose and walked down the stairs and into the crowd.

Jesus' face was troubled. He shook his head, his voice sad. "How hard it is for the rich to enter into eternal life."

Jesus turned and faced the steps crowded with people. He began a parable. As Nicodemus and his cousin listened, Joseph asked, "What makes his words so compelling?"

Nicodemus had asked himself that same question for several days now.

Jesus placed his hand on a man in ragged clothing and said, "Consider the lilies of the field, how they grow. They do not labor or spin. Yet I tell you that Solomon in all his glory was not dressed like one of these. If God so clothes the grass of the field, which is here today and tomorrow is thrown into the fire and burnt, how much more will he clothe you?"

Joseph leaned toward his cousin. "I'm beginning to understand why the people follow him."

Nicodemus replied, "And why the leaders fear him. I told you of my visit to Bethany. Three days ago when I went to meet him, I came away confused. Jesus said, 'One must be born again.' I have wondered at the meaning. Do I have to start again?" He pointed to the crowd below. "Do I have to be like these poor, unlearned souls?"

Joseph grimaced. "Did you hear what he said about the rich? He said 'it is harder for a camel to go through the eye of a needle than a rich man to enter the kingdom of heaven.'" He looked around his spacious, well appointed home. "I must admit I am wealthy. Last week Pontius Pilate gave my family permission to sell olive oil to this city. For me, it is a time of prosperity."

Nicodemus shook his head. "If the Jews gave up their riches, the Sanhedrin would be the first to feel it. He pulled on his outer cloak and fingered the designs around the hem. "The teachings of this Nazarene are hard. My heart loves and yet hates the purity and simplicity of his teachings. They bring both condemnation and hope. I still cannot accept him, but still ..."

*   *   *

The next week, news from Herod the Tetrarch's palace had a chilling effect on the Council. John the Baptizer was dead. A drunken Herod Antipas, tricked by his scheming mistress, Herodias, had ordered John's death. She requested his head on a platter to avenge his rebuke of her for leaving Philip, her previous husband.

Even though the Council had mixed reactions to John, they knew the people considered him a great prophet. His claims to be the forerunner of the Messiah had just increased the unrest. All of Israel was on edge.

Chapter Thirteen

Joseph

Joseph approached the Praetorian Gates.

The two guards moved to block his entrance. "You do not enter here without a summons, Jew." Their Aramaic was harsh and the last word was said with contempt.

"I am Joseph of Arimathea, and I have been bidden by Pontius Pilate. Here is my summons."

The guard studied the parchment. "Enter. The governor is in the chamber across the inner court."

Joseph climbed the four steps to the rounded stage called the place of judgment. He had watched Herod decree the death of forty young men from this very stage. Private trials were held in the inner court.

After entering the doorway, he walked through the tall plants decorating the courtyard. The pavement wound past marble fountains, and finally led to a single, ornate door. Another armored guard glanced at the pass and ushered him into the inner chamber. Pilate was seated at a desk facing the doorway. He was wearing a breastplate, polished to a silver brilliance. His hawk-like nose topped thin lips. His brows and head were shaved and his eyes were constantly shifting. His first words were abrupt. "You are the Jew who speaks the language of Rome?"

Joseph walked forward and dipped his head. "I speak the language of Rome and also of the Greeks. I was bidden by one of your officers. What is the reason for my summons?"

"Your Latin is good. You have been to Rome then?"

"I studied for eight years in the Roman school."

"Yet, you are a Jew, and the one who sells olive oil?"

Joseph gave a quick nod. "My father is the supplier of oil."

Pilate put his finger to his cheek. "Do I understand correctly, you are also a member of the Sanhedrin?"

"That is correct. They call me Joseph of Arimathea"

"Please, sit." Pilate clapped his hands. "Bring our guest something to drink." The woman attending him brought wine and set it before Joseph. "Joseph is our guest. He will be visiting us often. He speaks our language well and he has spent time in Rome." The woman bowed and Pilate touched her arm. "This is my wife, Procula."

Joseph had a strong desire to ask the reason for his summons but tried to remain patient.

Finally, Pilate leaned forward, and sighed. "I do not understand you Jews. You may have heard, but three weeks past, a throng of your people came to Caesarea to make demands of me. When I threatened them with death, they lay on the pavement and stated they would rather die than submit. All I wanted was money from your temple to build an aqueduct for this city. For their own good." He rose and paced. "I do not understand."

Joseph waited until he sat. "Yes, I am aware that may seem to you extreme. The reason for their action was that the money was corban."

His voice was cutting. "Corban, what's that?"

"It means 'given to God.' It cannot be used except for things of God."

"To me, getting clean water should be a godly pursuit." He slapped his palm on the desk. "Joseph, I need someone—a Jew—to explain these strange customs to me. The emperor wants peace in this land, and I will do my best. You can help me understand the workings of this Sanhedrin but, I don't want the high priest to know."

"Annas."

"Annas, yes, that's the old one. His son-in-law, the curly headed one?"

"Caiaphas, his new son-in-law."

"Once a week, I want you to come and tell me more about your strange people. My wife will also attend these sessions as well as two trusted counselors. For your help, I will guarantee your sole right to sell oil to our garrisons." He stood and took Joseph's hand.

Walking past the guards, Joseph grinned. He had made a big step toward becoming a very wealthy man. Now he could afford to build that home Rachel wanted.

*   *   *

In one month, the addition to Joseph's home in Arimathea was begun. Rachel began hiring builders, some from Caesarea. Her first pregnancy barely slowed her involvement.

Nicodemus, on a visit to Arimathea, watched the construction. He chided his cousin. "With a home here and in Jerusalem, you have become quite rich. Now I can brag that I have a rich relative."

Joseph chuckled and handed him a cup of wine. "Yes, and I have a beautiful wife to complete my bliss; you should consider ..." He watched Nicodemus' face, and changed the subject. "This Nazarene gains followers every day."

"And the Sadducees are becoming more determined to stop him."

Rachel joined the two men. "Tell me, my brother-in-law, what is this I hear of a Messiah in Galilee? My husband tells me little of the council events. Perhaps my close relative can inform me."

Nicodemus glanced at his cousin. Joseph chuckled and rose. "I have some work to oversee. You two go to the garden. That would be a good place to talk."

The two strolled to the trees beside the old home. In the shade, Rachel pulled two chairs close.

The informality of the setting loosened Nicodemus' tongue. He told her of his visit to Galilee and his night visit to Jesus in Bethany. Her deep-blue eyes searched his face. Talking to her, he found himself revealing more than he'd intended.

"And so, you have met this one, this Jesus? Do you believe he is the one we have waited for?" she asked.

Nicodemus pursed his lips. "I don't know, but he is a powerful figure."

She took his hand and squeezed it. "I will meet him." He looked into her eyes. He had no doubt she would meet this Jesus.

She confided, "I, too, am one who awaits the coming of the Messiah." She let go of Nicodemus' arm. "Thank you for telling me."

As she walked across the garden, Nicodemus shook his head. He wished he had a woman of this kind, even though he doubted he would find one with blue eyes. She was one of a kind.

* * *

Joseph's second visit to Pontius Pilate was a more relaxed occasion. The regent wore a loose-fitting toga instead of his armor. "Ah, my favorite Jew. Today I would like to hear more about your Council. I am told there are some distinct parties, and some are in contention with one another. Is this true?"

Joseph pulled his chair before the procurator. "It is true. Some don't believe in miracles or an afterlife, but are very politically connected. These are the Sadducees. Annas and Caiaphas follow these beliefs. At present, they are in a slight majority. The party of the Pharisees is the strict adherents of the Law, and many of those are priests and scribes. We have a few of the Herodians—a mixed lot—who want the return of the Herodian family to power."

"Are these the ones who want Herod to rule this land? I have not met the tetrarch, but it seems I must."

"The Herod in Galilee is no threat. He seems more involved in pleasing his new wife, Herodias, and entertaining himself, than seeking to expand his power."

"Herodias, I have heard of her. She was the wife of Herod's brother, Phillip, correct?"

Joseph was surprised. "Your information is correct."

Pilate leaned forward. "I also have heard of the death of one John the Baptist at her hands."

Joseph put a finger to his lips. This Roman legate had a sharp mind. "John was considered a prophet by our people. His death is very disturbing to most Jews."

"Aren't some of the Council Zealots? Those that seek to get rid of the Romans?"

Joseph shrugged. "If that is their sympathy, they do not let it be known. Perhaps some have that leaning."

Pilate touched his cheek. "And you, one who has been to Rome, you are a Pharisee?"

Joseph nodded. "Yes, my father whom I followed onto the Council, was also a Pharisee. We're just not as ... as radical."

"You have a leader in the Galilee district who is gathering great crowds to follow him. In fact, we have been watching him and his following. Do you consider him a threat to your country?"

Joseph stroked his chin. "The Sanhedrin is worried about him. Last month when he appeared at the Feast, he threw the money changers and merchants out of the temple. At times he seems violent, but most of the time he is quite gentle."

Pilate lifted his eyebrow. "And so, you have seen him?" His pale gray eyes searched Joseph for a reaction. "If you see him again, I want a detailed account, is that clear?"

Joseph left the meeting with the feeling that Pilate was not as ignorant of the land as he tried to seem.

*   *   *

Muriel was cleaning the table and humming her little tune as Nicodemus tried to concentrate on his writing. "Mother, what do you want to talk about?" He sighed and pulled another chair next to his and watched her.

"Son, since your father died and your sister left for the Galilee, it has just been the two of us." She took his hand. "You are now of that age ..."

He sighed. "Yes, Mother." He looked at her hair, streaked with gray. Wrinkles etched her face. "You are wondering if your son will ever make you a grandmother."

She bit her lip. "My son, many fine Jewish girls would love to find a handsome young man of your position to marry." She took his other hand. "Now I understand that the youngest daughter of Gamaliel is almost your age, is ..."

"Mother, her name is Deborah, she is over ten years younger, and just like her wise namesake, is never at a loss for words. She is a forthright young woman. We have met, but I don't think she is interested in marriage."

"In our land every girl is interested in marriage." She stroked the back of his hand. "Just consider it."

Nicodemus kissed his mother's forehead. "For you, my mother, I will consider it. But you must promise one thing."

Muriel brow arched. "Fine, what thing?"

"I do not need a matchmaker, especially my mother." He studied her face and narrowed his eyes. "Have you already met her?"

Muriel blushed. "We merely talked."

* * *

The spring flowers were in full bloom and the hills around Jerusalem were green. Gamaliel's garden was awash in flowers of all colors. His wife and Deborah were dutifully serving refreshments. The old teacher carefully trimmed some blooming plants beside the table. "God is great and he blesses us with his flowers. We should delight in the precious gifts of His creation." He turned to his guest. "Nicodemus, my daughter is one of incisive mind and often too quick a tongue. She is my harshest critic and most loyal supporter."

Deborah exhaled and shook her head at Nicodemus. "My father seems to be leading to one of his famous questions. He is probably going to embarrass both of us by suggesting that we get to know each other better. I saw your mother and my father talking several days ago. They became silent when I entered the room. My assumption was the conversation concerned us." She turned to her father. "For your information, Father, I consider Nicodemus an attractive man, and I would be pleased to have him as a suitor, does this please you?"

Nicodemus almost dropped his drink. Gamaliel, for the first time Nicodemus recalled, looked startled. Nicodemus managed a grin to match the one on Deborah's face.

*   *   *

In the following weeks, the relationship moved quickly and Nicodemus found himself spending more evenings at Gamaliel's home than his own.

One evening, he stood before his mother, who was sewing in her favorite chair. He leaned toward her. "Mother, how would you like to have a daughter-in-law?"

Muriel was briefly speechless. Recovering her poise, she placed her sewing aside. "One must consider the importance of such a thing."

Nicodemus chided. "Mother, you were the one who said I was old enough to seek a wife. I am also old enough to make those decisions for myself." He kissed her on the forehead and teased. "We have decided to name our second daughter after you."

Muriel gasped. "You have talked of such things this soon?" She went back to her sewing, a crinkle touching her cheek.

*   *   *

Later, in the jungle behind the home that served Gamaliel as a household retreat, Deborah faced Nicodemus. "My parents are concerned that I am rushing our betrothal, but I have assured them we are both prepared to face the task of marriage. I am sure ... are you?"

Nicodemus took her hands and squeezed them. "I have never been more certain of anything."

"My father tells me that you have been to Galilee. Tell me what it's like, and did you swim in the lake? I understand it's beautiful."

"Yes, I swam in the cold blue waters of that sea, and it's gorgeous. I also swam in the warm Mediterranean. Why do you ask?"

Deborah pulled him to a bench and sat close. "You must promise me, someday you will teach me to swim. I don't want to live my whole life within the walls of this city. I want to see the ocean and the Sea of Galilee. I want to climb Mount Tabor like Deborah the Judge once did. I want to stand on the summit and imagine how she stood and looked out on thousands of Midianite warriors. I want to stand on the summit of Mount Sinai, just like Moses did."

Nicodemus watched excitement light her face. "I have an uncle who lives on the beach at Caesarea. He would graciously invite us to be his guests. Would you like our wedding night to be there gazing out on the ocean?"

"Is it really on the beach?" She bit her lip. "And will you really take me swimming?"

Nicodemus tried to remember whether he'd ever seen a woman swim before. But had he ever met a woman as bold as this one? "My love, I will promise you. Not only will I teach you to swim, I will climb Mount Tabor with you, and any other mountains you choose."

Deborah planted a gentle kiss on his cheek. "Then, my love, let us get on with our plans."

Nicodemus, forgetting his usual reserve, took Deborah in his arms and kissed her. "I am sure—I want to be your husband, and I would like to marry you, soon."

She held him close, her body warm against his. "And I promise you, I will bring you pleasure, and will always be there for you." She looked into his eyes. "And I will speak the truth, no matter how difficult that might be."

Nicodemus looked into her intense dark eyes. He was sure she would do exactly that.

Two weeks later, at the meeting of the council, Gamaliel announced the forthcoming marriage of Deborah and Nicodemus. Joseph was the first to congratulate his cousin.

*   *   *

Upon Zedekiah's invitation and Deborah's insistence, their wedding—originally planned as a small celebration on the beach at Caesarea—grew each day. Ziva and Miriam could hardly believe the number of people attending. Finally Ziva and Muriel gave up trying to seat everyone, and most sat on the soft sand. The ocean waves gently serenaded the guests.

The blue *chuppah* canopy flapped gently in the ocean breeze as Uncle Zedekiah, dressed in his finest blue silk, presided. His blue sash matched his yarmulke, which accented his white hair. His bass voice was strong above the soft lapping of the waves, as he began the *Kiddushin.* "This is the sacred ceremony of spiritual binding our God has given us in the Torah. God said that man and woman should be fruitful and multiply. This is *Mitzvah,* a divine precept. And now, by the rights granted unto man to take a woman to be his God-given help-meet, do you, Nicodemus bar-Barak, receive Deborah daughter of Gamaliel to be your espoused bride? To cherish this one, who by your side will help and strengthen you as long as you both shall walk upon this earth?

Nicodemus stood looking at his bride almost in a daze. Her long white gown was bordered in gold trim which matched the soft cap on her head. Her dark hair and eyes contrasted with the gown which moved in the soft sea-breeze. Joseph, standing beside him, nudged him. He jumped and blurted, "I will."

Zedekiah smiled. "And do you, Deborah, daughter of Gamaliel bar Hillel, accept this man to this *Ketuvch* that binds you to this man for as long as God grants you life?"

Deborah stated clearly, "As God is my witness, I accept Nicodemus as my God-given husband, to honor and uphold for all my life."

"As King Solomon wisely wrote, we are made stronger with a friend at our side. You have both found one to strengthen you and support you. Solomon also wrote, 'A three-strand cord is not easily broken. God is that third strand. Do you have a symbol of this bond?"

Nicodemus took the simple gold band and slipped it on Deborah's finger.

Zedekiah took the blue cloth from his shoulders and draped it across their joined hands. "This union is *Ketuvch.*

Joseph and Rachel stepped forward to sign the scroll that Zedekiah handed them. "And now the *Ketuvch is sealed.*"

Zedekiah raised his arm. "And now by the authority granted by almighty God, it is my solemn pleasure to announce that you have been joined by the mighty power of God. From this day forward let no man divide this sacred union asunder." He lifted his hands. "*Lechaim!*"

The crowd shouted, "*Lechaim!*"

The couple kissed and Joseph held his bride a long time as the waves rolled up the warm beach.

The *Bedekin* filled the spacious room with celebrating guests that spilled out to the courtyard and even down to the beach. The Cantor's voice was strong as he serenaded the newly-weds and their guests. Fortunately Ziva had stocked plenty of food and the wine flowed freely. It was late before the two were led to their *chader yichud*.

Their wedding chamber was a wing of his uncle's home and the room was awash in red and gold. Flowers were in vases on an entire side of the room and their scent filled the room. The one large window was open to the evening sky and the last golden rays bounced on the incoming waves. Nicodemus' arms encircled his bride as they watched the setting sun.

Deborah turned and held both his hands, her gaze steady. "My husband, I promise to bring you happiness. This is the most wonderful evening of my life. I shall always remember this time, and this place."

Nicodemus took her face gently. His fingers touched her lips. His kiss was long and passionate.

Chapter Fourteen

Disciples

In the cleft between the anti-Lebanese mountains and the slopes of Gadara, the deep blue of the Sea of Galilee sparkled. Joanna sat among the growing crowd of people. Most were country people, mainly poor, many with ailments. Jesus stood before a woman who was writhing in agony. Her hair was matted, her mouth frothed in white, and her eyes stared blankly at the Nazarene. Jesus' voice boomed, "Come out of her, you demonic spirits. Leave her in peace." The woman convulsed, her whole body contorting and trembling. Within minutes the convulsion stopped and she lay still.

"She's dead," someone wailed. The crowd stood in quiet shock.

Jesus bent, his hand stroked her forehead. "Bring some water, and some of you women attend to her."

The woman opened her eyes and her lips moved silently.

Joanna knelt and unfastened the sash around her own waist. She wiped the woman's now peaceful face. Another woman brought water. Together, they cleaned the streaked face.

Within a few minutes the woman sat up. Her eyes were bright with tears. "My mind is clear, they are gone ...all gone. Praise God." She turned to the smiling Jesus. "Thank you ... thank you, sir."

The crowd noise increased with sounds of amazement. "She's healed! Mary of Magdalene is in her right mind."

"Jesus healed her!"

"God has visited her on this day."

Jesus lifted her to her feet. "God has chosen you as his special minister. See to it that you use your healing to glorify his name."

Mary proclaimed, "From this day forward I will serve you. May I glorify him, as your servant?" She dropped to her knees before Jesus. Joanna pulled a small brush from her belt pouch and brushed Mary's hair.

Jesus looked into her face, smiled, and raised her to her feet. "You, Mary, will glorify my Father in you life."

Later, the two women walked together into Capernaum. Reaching a house near the lake, Joanna invited Mary inside. "This is the home of Chuza, steward to Herod. He is seldom here, but mainly spends his time with the tetrarch. Chuza and I are espoused to be married sometime this year. He is a good man, and you will be welcome to stay until you are well."

Mary sat on the bed, her countenance glowing. "For three years I have had these seizures, and seven demons were fighting in my mind ... I couldn't stop them. My friends have deserted me and my family given me up. This is such a blessed day. She jumped to her feet and embraced Joanna. I know now, I'm completely healed. I have been touched by the Master."

Joanna brought some bread and milk to Mary. "Take these and I will wash your feet while you eat. This is a day we will both remember all our lives."

"Are you a follower of Jesus?"

"From this time onward," Joanna affirmed, "I am."

*   *   *

Two days' journey to the south, the complete Sanhedrin Council filled the chamber.

Caiaphas lifted his staff for silence. "Within this past year the Nazarene has filled the countryside with his false teaching and tricks. He has sent bands throughout the land and brought bad reports about us to the people. He professes to be the Messiah and yet blasphemes our holy temple." He glared around the assembly. "We have issued this statement to all the Jerusalem synagogues." He unrolled a parchment, and cleared his throat. "Let it be known to all followers of Jehovah in Israel: Anyone who admits believing that this false messiah, Jesus of Nazareth, is God's son, will be cast out of the synagogue. This is the proclamation of the Council of the Sanhedrin." He glared at the court, and rolled the parchment.

Nicodemus stood, his heart pounding. Caiphas and the Council would not violate this innocent Nazarene any longer. It was his first time to address the entire assembly. "Does our law condemn a man we have never heard?" There was dead silence in the chamber. Caiaphas and Annas glared at him, and then turned, whispering to one another. Most on either side of the Council just stared at him. He couldn't read their thoughts, but he knew—from now on he would be marked as one who stood against the priesthood.

As the assembly adjourned, Gamaliel strolled next to Nicodemus. "My son-in-law, you have just become a new target of the hatred of the chief priests. I hope you are prepared for what may follow."

That evening, Deborah sat across the table from Nicodemus. "My father told me about the meeting today." Her face showed no emotion, but her dark eyes searched his face. "You do know that as a ruler of the largest synagogue in the city, your position and salary may have vanished?"

"Perhaps it is time for another leader to take my place, and we can go to a smaller synagogue." He listened to the falling rain. "My father was one of the original ten that formed that synagogue. I have served it since his death."

"And you have served it well, my husband. It is one of the most prosperous in the city."

"God will provide." He poured a glass of wine for both. "And you, my wife, what are your thoughts?"

"I do not believe in this healer at this time, but ..." She took a long drink. "But, I am your wife. I will always be."

* * *

It was cold. Often fall in Jerusalem brought cold winds. Nicodemus pulled his heavy mantle close. The crowd was smaller at this Feast of Tabernacles. No one knew if the Nazarene would appear, but they were halfway through the festival and no one had seen him.

Nicodemus stood watching the worshipers move across the upper court.

Joseph joined him. "Cousin, it was good to see you at our congregation last Sabbath. Our small synagogue can use more good teachers."

"It was hard to leave our old congregation. I had overseen it for many years. But, yes, it was time for me to move on."

A band of priests rushed across the courtyard. He heard one exclaim. "He's come; the Nazarene is in the lower courtyard." Nicodemus and Joseph hurried to join the others. By the time they reached the stairs, a large crowd had gathered. Jesus stood with a circle of disciples at the foot of the staircase.

They moved closer to hear his words. "My teaching is not my own. It comes from him who sent me. If anyone chooses to do God's will, he will find out whether my teaching comes from God or whether I speak on my own." Jesus ended his words pointing to the priests. "Why are you trying to kill me?"

Ahaz bellowed, "Who is trying to kill you, are you mad?"

Someone near Nicodemus whispered, "Isn't this the one they are trying to arrest? Here he is speaking publicly."

Another replied, "Do the priests believe in him too?"

A commotion erupted from the eastern gate. A squad of guards, Caiaphas and his friends in the center, were almost dragging a woman across the yard. The woman was trying to hold a small blanket to cover her nakedness, but the guards held her firmly. Finally the guards pushed the crowd away and threw the trembling woman before Jesus. One of the priests demanded of Jesus. "This woman was caught in the act of adultery, the very act. The law says that we are to stone such a one." Everything became deathly silent. "What do you say?" The woman clutched the meager garment as close as she could. Nicodemus watched a man shift the stone in his hand and he wondered what Jesus would say.

Jesus bent and wrote in the dust of the ground.

Another priest asked, "What do you say?"

The crowd stood silent, even Jesus' followers froze. Jesus rose and looked squarely at Caiaphas. "Let him who is without sin cast the first stone." He then bent down and again began to write. There was a protracted silence, several looked at one another.

The sound of a rock dropping into the dirt was followed by another, and another. The crowd began to leave, the older ones first.

Finally Caiaphas threw his stone to the ground, turned and strode away.

Jesus rose and faced the woman. She lifted her face to look into his eyes. It was only then that Nicodemus recognized her. Her heavy make-up was streaked, one ornate ear-ring missing—it was Cloe, the girl from the market now grown into ...this.

Jesus asked gently, "Where are your accusers?"

She sobbed. "All gone, my Lord."

He took her hand and looked into her face. "Go your way and sin no more."

A woman stepped forward and put a cloak around Cloe's shoulders and placed her arm around her. Nicodemus' mouth fell open—the woman was his sister, Joanna.

Joseph and Nicodemus walked behind two guards who were headed toward the Sanhedrin's chambers. The temple guards had barely crossed the portal when the voice of Annas demanded. "Where is he, why didn't you arrest him?"

One tall guard shook his head. "No one ever spoke the way this man does."

Annas bellowed, "You mean he deceived you also? Have any of the rulers of the Pharisees believed in him?"

Nicodemus blinked, perhaps one of the Pharisees did believe, maybe more.

Three days later, the Sanhedrin met. It was almost impossible for Annas to quiet the assembly, with arguments nearly ending in blows. Finally gaining control, he announced that the called session was to examine a clear case of Sabbath violation. Members grumbled as they took their places.

Guards escorted a shabbily dressed man before the Council.

Ahaz, the chief inquisitor, asked, "And you say you were blind and now you see? How did that happen?"

"A man put mud on my eyes. He told me to go and wash in the pool of Siloam. Now, I see."

Ahaz stood before the man and shouted. "This Jesus is not from God, he does not keep the Sabbath."

The man shook his head. "How can a sinner do such miraculous signs?"

Another argument erupted among the Council members.

After order was restored, Ahaz demanded, "What do you say about him? It was your eyes he opened." His voice quavered as he spoke.

One other whispered, "Who indeed can restore the sight of one born blind?

The man spread his hands. "He is a prophet."

Caiaphas stood. "Bring in this man's parents."

Nicodemus whispered to Joseph. "Look, I know them; they are from my old synagogue."

Caiaphas sat and glared at the older couple. "Is this your son, the one born blind? How is it that he now can see?"

The old man's voice was halting. "We know he is our son, he was born blind. We do not know how he now sees." He looked around the room. "He is of age, ask him."

Joseph whispered to Nicodemus. "That man knows, if he acknowledges Jesus is God's son, he too will be thrown out of the synagogue."

Annas frowned at the couple. "Give glory to God, we know this man is a sinner."

The man who was blind spoke up. "One thing I know, I was blind, now I see."

Caiaphas stood beside his father-in-law. "How did he open your eyes?"

The man stroked his chin, his voice calm. "I told you once and you did not listen, do you want to become his disciples, too?"

Bedlam broke out. Nicodemus hardly kept from laughing as Caiaphas signaled the guards to take the three—the blind man and his parents—out.

As the healed man left, he turned and shouted. "Nobody has ever heard of one opening the eyes of one born blind. If this man were not from God he could do nothing!"

Chapter Fifteen

Bethany

Joanna trudged up the hill, the moon lighting the path ahead. Her burden, wrapped in a shawl, was covered like one would bundle a baby. She looked at the little armful and a heavy sadness surged through her heart—a reminder of the child she had never born for Nathan. They were married only two months before he was arrested. Now, with her betrothal to Chuza, and their years, she doubted if she would have a child of her own. No! She would not let her mind go there. She adjusted the small blanket over her burden, the white alabaster glistening in the dim light. Reaching the crest of the hill, she studied the faint lights shining from the homes of the town. She mumbled, "Third on the left, a stone archway." Her little armful cuddled carefully, she walked to the door.

One knock and the door opened. A man near the age of her brother answered. "Yes?" he studied her face. "Who do you seek?"

Joanna whispered, "Is this the home of Mary and Martha?"

The man glanced at the path. "Why do you seek us?"

From behind the man a voice called. "Joanna, is that you? What are you doing in Judea?" Mary pushed by her brother and embraced Joanna. She turned to him. "Lazarus, this is one of the disciples from

Galilee. She is one who attends the Master. Come in, come in. It's getting cold. We have a fire going." She studied the small bundle in Joanna's arms. "A child?"

Joanna shook her head and handed the bundle to Lazarus. He took off the shawl and stroked the gleaming white alabaster jar. Joanna dropped to a couch while Mary examined the cruse.

Mary's gaze posed the question. "Is this a gift?"

Joanna rubbed her arm. "The jar is something belonging to Jesus. It has been with my family since his birth." She rubbed her hands together. "May I have something warm? The evening is chill."

Mary moved quickly to the kettle hanging near the glowing fire. "Forgive me, I was just so excited to see you. We will warm our herbal beverage. Would you like fresh honey?"

Joanna rubbed her arms. "Thank you. Until a month ago, I was with Jesus in Galilee. When we came to the Feast of Tabernacles, I was staying with my mother in Jerusalem." She accepted the drink from Mary. "I need to explain the gift. My brother, Nicodemus, is in Arimathea helping with the olive pressing. Yesterday, guards came from the temple—they were seeking Jesus. It frightened my mother terribly. This cruse was sitting on our hearth, as it has been since the time it was left with us for safe keeping. The soldiers looked at it, but didn't ask. Fortunately, the engraving was not turned toward them or it may have caused more trouble." She tasted the drink Mary handed her.

Lazarus' fingers traced over the engraving, and a puzzled look covered his face.

Joanna sipped the drink. "My father, who died ten years past, etched those words on it when I was only fourteen. He wanted everyone to know it was a special gift."

Lazarus frowned. "The words—for Messiah—I don't understand."

"It happened in Bethlehem some thirty years ago. Mary and Joseph of Nazareth, expecting their firstborn, journeyed to Bethlehem. They came because of the census. The baby was born a day later. During that time there were many signs, a wondrous star, and shepherds telling of visiting angels. Shortly after that, camels came from the east. Wise men were seeking the child they said was to be the new king. They brought gold, this cruse of nard and large bags of frankincense and myrrh. Joseph, Jesus' father, was warned to take the child to Egypt to escape Herod's wrath. When they left, my father promised to keep this cruse and the bag in trust until they returned.

"Was this the time of the killing of the babies in Bethlehem?"

Joanna choked out the words. "My little brother died by a Roman blade." She took a deep breath. "Joseph and Mary never returned to Bethlehem. Now, with the danger in Jerusalem from the Jews ..."

Mary ran her fingers over the smooth white stone. "We will keep it for him. It's Nard? That's very expensive."

"My father said it was worth over a half year's wages. Mother and I thought the jar would be safe here, since the Jews only searched Jerusalem. I knew Jesus came here often ... I thought ..."

Mary frowned. "Jesus is aware the Jews are trying to kill him. He has gone to the Jordan, we don't know where, but he will probably come back ... perhaps at Passover."

"Won't that be dangerous?"

Mary glanced at her brother. "Once, in this very room, he told his disciples that he must suffer and be persecuted. I think he also told your brother when he visited us a year ago, about the trials to come. We, like you, will hold this in trust for him."

*   *   *

The sun was sinking over the haze across the Shannon Valley and the hills around Arimathea were ablaze with the red-yellow hues of autumn. Nicodemus was tired, a different tired. His muscles ached, but his mind was clear—not like when he listened to the endless theological bantering of the priests. Working at an olive press was a joy he hadn't experienced since youth. He pulled the dirty apron off and hung it on its peg in the shed. With satisfaction he counted the full barrels. He and the men had filled twelve barrels of Arimathea's best olive oil in one day. Joseph would be pleased. He walked to the well basin and stripped off his upper shirt. He gasped when the cold water hit his skin. He doused himself again. It was the same chilling joy he felt plunging into the Sea of Galilee so many years ago.

Joseph called from the house that dinner was prepared. Nicodemus dried himself on the towels hanging near the basin. He shook the dust off his shirt, dressed, and headed toward the house. Joseph's new home adjoining his father's was built in a stylish Roman manner. The large columned porch and flowering plants had been planned by Rachel.

Nicodemus found working in the olive oil good for his soul. He contemplated convincing Deborah to join him on his next trip. Since their marriage, she had not left the city. His wife needed to get to know Rachel and Joseph.

Rachel greeted him with a warm smile and a freshly cleaned shirt. "If you'd like to change before dinner?" Her hint made him chuckle. He took the clean garment, moved around the corner of the porch, and changed. He hardly finished when the dinner chime— Rachel's innovation—sounded. As he rounded the porch, he stopped and watched Joseph's little son playing with a kitten. He and Deborah were not blessed with a child and, already, Rachel was showing signs of a new pregnancy.

The whole family surrounded the table. Uncle Joram led the prayer. Nicodemus was reminded of his own father's eloquence as his uncle asked the blessings. Joram's beard was entirely white. A cane lay at his side, but his words were still concise.

Halfway through the meal, the dogs outside began barking. Joseph rose. Soon, a hired servant ushered an armored soldier into the room. Joseph greeted the Roman as one he knew well, and invited him to join them.

"This is my family, Cracius. My wife is the pretty one, the mistress of my home. My father is a former member of the Council. The tired looking one on the end is my cousin, Nicodemus, who is also a member of the Sanhedrin." He finished the introductions as the Roman removed his helmet. His brow was covered with sweat. "Cracius, would you join us at dinner?"

"I come with a message from Pontius Pilate." He bowed to Rachel. "I thank you for the invitation, but I stopped in the village and have already eaten."

Nicodemus was startled. Joseph had just invited a non-Jew to eat with them, but this Roman seemed aware this was against the custom of the Jews.

Cracius turned to Joseph. "Tomorrow we need your skill as we question a prisoner. Barabbas, the insurrectionist, was captured. Pilate will begin at noon tomorrow." He bowed slightly. "I am sorry to call you away from this pleasant gathering."

Joseph sighed. "Tell the governor I'll come."

The soldier saluted, turned and strode out.

* * *

Joseph studied the face of Barabbas. He was known to all Judea, and was said to have killed many men. His face and arms showed the lash marks and one eye was blackened, and almost closed. Blood from his wounds seeped through his dirty tunic. He smelled foul.

The centurion briefed Joseph on his capture. "A small detachment of soldiers had been patrolling the canyons leading from Jerusalem to Jericho when a man was spotted entering a high cave above the roadway. Two soldiers were sent to investigate and a group of bandits attacked them. After a fierce sword battle with casualties on both sides, we captured this man."

Pontius Pilate, dressed in his bright armor, strode into the room and took his place on the podium chair. "And now, my not so noble rebel, we have questions to ask. Should you refuse, as you tried to do yesterday, you will be beaten until you die. Is this clear?"

He turned to Joseph, and Joseph translated Pilate's question into Aramaic.

After translation, Barabbas' head dipped.

Pilate gestured to Joseph. "This man is a fellow Jew and he will direct my questions. Your attempts to act as though you don't understand will not work."

Joseph saw the look in Barabbas' good eye—he understood too well. Pilate asked rather general questions and Barabbas answered.

When Pilate inquired about their reasons for resistance, Barabbas launched into a tirade which Pilate interrupted before Joseph could translate.

Pilate pointed his finger at the prisoner, his voice icy. "You Jews have no rights, certainly not the right to rob and murder innocent people of any race." His finger pointed like a javelin. "You are nothing but a thief and a murderer!"

Joseph didn't try to interpret, Barabbas seem to catch the meaning.

"And now, you scum, I want to know who supplied you with all of the weapons and food that have kept your miserable band of rogues from starving in that desert hole."

Joseph had only started translating when Barabbas stood straight and shook his head.

Pilate abruptly rose. "This rebel will rot in prison until he gives me information. I seek names. Also, remind him of our means of extracting information." Barabbas was jerked toward the door, his ankle chains rattling. Before the door slammed behind him, Pilate barked at the centurion, "

Give him adequate food; I want him to live until we have discovered what he knows. I don't want him dead ... just yet."

Pilate sat again and addressed Joseph, his voice calm. "I need you to perform a special task for me. Many reports are coming to my attention about the Nazarene who is exciting your people. My informants tell me he is now on the Jordan with great crowds of followers. He doesn't seem to be preparing them for rebellion, but he needs watching. I would like for you to go, with a couple of my trusted men, to the valley and observe him for a few weeks." He tossed a bag of coins to Joseph. "Two month's of silver are in the pouch. That should cover your needs. I want to know how much of a threat this Jew poses."

Joseph opened the pouch; it was filled with silver. He closed the bag and stroked his beard. "If I am to act as a spy among these disciples of Jesus it would be better if no Roman accompanied me. May I suggest, Your Excellency, my cousin, who is also a member of the Council, journey with me?"

Pilate interlocked his fingers and bent forward. "Yes, it might be wise to take one of the Council with you." He smacked his fist into his palm. "The followers of this Jesus would think it was the Sanhedrin watching them and not the Romans. Very wise, Joseph." His eyes searched Joseph. "Have you, by chance, met this Nazarene?"

Joseph shook his head. "I've never met him, but I have seen him at a distance."

That was about to change.

Chapter Sixteen

Jordan

The rugged cliffs along the road closed in on the two men. The temperature rose as they descended into the parched Jordan Rift. The cliffs of crumbling mud were broken by strips of red and dirty-yellow rock. Withered clumps of grass struggled to survive the dryness.

Joseph glanced nervously at the dark caves high above the roadway. He turned to Nicodemus who was stuffing his cloak into the bag slung over his shoulder. "I wonder if there are eyes watching us from those cliffs up there."

Nicodemus wiped the sweat from his brow. "Today, many travelers are going to Jericho. I think the outlaws prefer lone victims when the light is dim. However, I do think we should stop this evening at the inn. We should not be on this road after dark. Also, I'm hungry."

Joseph ventured, "While we were in Jerusalem, did I overhear Muriel and you arguing? She sounded very upset."

Nicodemus kicked a stone. "My mother is having difficulty with my being forced from our synagogue. My father was a part of that congregation's beginning, and I followed his role as leader. This move by the Council to call my loyalty in question has changed her relationships with a synagogue where she grew up. She cannot leave the congregation, yet she feels the stares, and hears the gossip. I can become a part of another synagogue, but my mother ..." He shook his head.

"How is Deborah with all this?"

"My wife is loyal, yet leaving the flock her parents are a part of hurt her deeply. She's not spoken of it to me."

Joseph stopped and faced his cousin. "We are soon to be among the followers of Jesus. From what we have seen of his miracles, and what you and I have heard, I am becoming convinced this one is the Messiah. You have not told me of your decisions since your visit to see him. What do you think? Is he the one we have waited for?"

Nicodemus' face wrinkled. "When I went to him in Bethany, I went seeking ..." He shook his head. "I'm not really sure what I was seeking, but after he said I needed to, to be born again, I have asked myself many times what he meant. I am a teacher of the Torah, a member of the Sanhedrin. My family is one of the leading upholders of the Law." His face showed the torture of his conflict. He turned and trudged off down the roadway, his sandals shuffling the red dust.

Joseph watched his cousin slump ahead. He examined his own thoughts. Who was this Jesus anyway? He certainly had caused a cloud of uncertainty in their world—and in the minds of two men who were trained to know the answers.

* * *

The next morning, they arrived at Jericho before the coolness of the morning had disappeared. The mist was rising from the Dead Sea and Joseph could see Mount Nebo in the distance. Joseph wondered if Moses, standing on its summit ages ago and viewing this land, could have imagined what it had become—a conquered nation ruled by half Jews and a priesthood descended from every tribe and belief.

He turned to Nicodemus. "Do you suppose the great Lawgiver, when he spoke of the prophet to come, ever envisioned someone poor like the Nazarene being the Messiah? Or one who is so opposed to the high priesthood?"

Nicodemus bit his cheek, but he merely shook his head.

"On the other hand, many of our prophets were from humble backgrounds, and were opposed by the priesthood even then. I even find myself opposed to many of our priesthood." Since his cousin didn't seem interested in replying, he continued. "These miracles he performs cannot be anything else than the power of the Almighty. Even though he doesn't fit the pattern we had expected, more and more I am becoming convinced."

Nicodemus blurted, "Are you becoming a believer in this Nazarene?" He had not been so angry at Joseph since childhood.

They were nearing Jericho. The crowds flooded the road to the north leading up the Jordan valley. Both men, though not wearing any of their priestly adornments, stood out. Most in the crowd were poor, many ragged. From their conversations, it was obvious they were all seeking the Nazarene.

By midday, they found themselves walking down the banks of the Jordan toward a throng of people assembled at the water's edge. Joseph recognized the sons of Zebedee and waved to John. A dozen men were clumped around Pete and the woman he had just baptized. Others stood on the bank, waiting to enter the water. John was jubilant as he approached the two.

Joseph studied him. "My, since our time in Capernaum you've grown tall. You remember Nicodemus, don't you?"

John chuckled. "How could I ever forget my old teacher, one who made me learn to study very hard? One I will always love and appreciate." He kissed Nicodemus on both cheeks. "Welcome, Rabbi. It has been too long. Both of you, come. There is someone you need to meet. That is, after we have something to eat."

Nicodemus stiffened. He knew who John meant. Was he ready to face the man who'd confused him more than anyone he'd ever met?

"Jesus is alone praying, but he will return soon."

The cousins followed John upstream to a grassy flat where women were preparing food. The smell of roasting lamb filled the air and the smoke drifted over the river. John's brother, James, joined them and kissed both men in greeting.

Someone shouted, "Nicodemus, my brother!" He turned just as Joanna threw her arms around him.

"I didn't know you were here. Mother wondered where you had gone. It is good to see you, you look—"

She laughed. "Just say I look happy. I am indeed blessed. But come, join us in bread. You too, cousin. What brings our distinguished guests to our humble camp, or should I guess?"

Sitting on the sparse grass, they were all talking when several disciples turned toward a figure that had just arrived. Joanna rose, her face radiant.

"My Lord."

All stood to greet the Nazarene.

Jesus had a hint of a grin on his face as he moved toward Nicodemus. His first words shook Nicodemus to his core. "And who is the Son of Man, Nicodemus?" He took a dish with bread and lamb and thanked the women serving him. "Have you two come to observe how these are being born of the water?" He paused and looked into their eyes. "Or perhaps, there is another reason you have come." Nicodemus felt a chill as the Nazarene studied them.

Other disciples joined the circle around Jesus. Peter greeted the cousins. "Ah, I see we have guests from the temple." His grip was as strong as ever as he shook their hands. "We welcome you both. I learned much during our time in the Galilee. You both will learn much more from our teacher." The followers were in no hurry to eat. Their laughter filled the air. Joanna tucked her long skirt beneath her as sat beside her brother.

Jesus plucked a seed from an overhanging limb and held it for all to see. The disciples quieted expectantly. "A seed must fall to the earth and die, and thus it springs to new life." He looked around the listeners. "And so it will be with the Son of Man."

Peter muttered, "May it never be."

Jesus must have heard the reply. He sadly shook his head.

That evening under the stars, Joanna, breathing heavily, slept beside her brother.

Nicodemus adjusted the pack under his head and tried to find a comfortable position.

Joseph spoke softly. "Tomorrow I am going to seek baptism."

Nicodemus sat up. "You are a believer then that this man is the Messiah, God's Son?" He exhaled. "Have you counted the cost? What about your family?"

Joseph rose to one elbow and faced his cousin. "I have seen the miracles and heard his teaching. Jesus fulfills prophecy, yet there is more. I believe ... I believe he is the one we have waited for. Tomorrow, I will become a follower." He laid back. "Whatever it may cost, I will follow."

Nicodemus said nothing. A lump was in his throat. That night he tried to sleep but, long into the night, he lay awake. He listened to Joanna's restful breathing. The words of Jesus flashed through his mind. "The wind blows where it will. We hear the sound and we do not know where it comes from or where it is going. So is one born of the Spirit." He tried timing his breath to her slow breath and was soon asleep.

*   *   *

John guided Joseph into the slightly muddy water. "It gets deeper near the middle." He paused mid-stream. Both men were wearing only their light undergarments. Nicodemus didn't hear his next words, but John placed one hand on Joseph's back and raised his other, fingers spread to the sky. He put his hand over Joseph's mouth and pushed him backward into the waist-deep water. Joseph came up dripping. He grabbed John in a bear hug.

A cheer erupted from the shore, but Nicodemus felt a burst of anger. He hoped his frustration wasn't apparent to the others who stood near. He turned and saw he was merely an arms length from the face of Jesus.

After a moment of silence, Jesus spoke. "Often faith comes quickly, like the simple joys of a child. With others, it demands a struggle reaching deep into the very soul."

When Joseph reached the shore, he was surrounded by others congratulating and welcoming him to the fellowship. He finally found Nicodemus and walked to him. Nicodemus looked around. Jesus was gone.

Joseph grinned. "Cousin, today I feel as free as a bird, or like a youth at play." He regarded Nicodemus' troubled face. "My belief grabbed my heart as we watched an unlearned man, one born blind, confound the best minds of our Council and see the change the

Nazarene brought to his life. We have seen four healings here on this river. Jesus' words stymied the best minds of the Sanhedrin, and yet his teaching reaches the masses. What more would the Messiah do?"

Nicodemus shook his head. He had witnessed the healings. He'd heard the teachings. Still he was not ready to face what it might mean in his life—in the life of his whole family.

That evening, with the disciples gathered around, Jesus taught. They were listening to him when a servant of Lazarus of Bethany stumbled into camp. He dropped to his knees before Jesus. "Lazarus is very sick. Mary and Martha pray you, please come, it is desperate."

Surprisingly, Jesus seemed unmoved.

Andrew, looking puzzled, blurted, "Jesus, Lazarus and his sisters are your loyal followers. Aren't you concerned?"

Jesus replied to the disciples, "Lazarus' sickness will not end in death. No, it is for God's glory." He touched the servant. "Stay with us until the time is fulfilled."

The servant looked dumfounded, but remained silent.

Peter asked, "Lord, don't you love Lazarus?"

The next two days were full of baptisms, teaching and fellowship. There was still a feeling of confusion concerning Lazarus but then Jesus startled the camp by announcing. "Let us go back to Judea, Lazarus has fallen asleep."

Nicodemus watched as the apostles huddled around Jesus.

James blurted, "If he is asleep he will waken."

Jesus slowly opened his palm. "Lazarus is dead."

The apostles looked at one-another in shocked silence.

"We will go to Bethany."

Peter frowned. "They're seeking to kill you there."

Jesus replied, "Are there not twelve hours of daylight for us to do God's work?"

Thomas threw his arms in the air. "Come, let's go and die with him."

Chapter Seventeen

Lazarus

John dropped back to walk with Nicodemus and Joseph. "Jesus seems in a hurry today, but it is nice to get out of that Jordan Valley. This cool breeze is refreshing."

Joseph put his arm around the apostle. "After my baptism three days ago, I almost picked you up and danced with you. I have not experienced such elation in years."

John burst out in laughter. "You mean dance in the middle of the Jordan? We would have looked silly." Wrinkles etched his tanned face. "It would have been all right, I suppose. We both felt the joy of the Spirit."

Hollowness filled Nicodemus as he listening to the two. He said nothing—he didn't feel joy. Confusion nagged his soul. Joseph had accepted—why couldn't he?

Approaching the road to Bethany, Nicodemus quizzed John. "Jesus and Lazarus were very close?"

"Mary, Martha and Lazarus always opened their home to us. Jesus once said, 'The foxes have holes, the birds have nests, but the Son of Man doesn't have a place to lay his head.' When we were near the home of Lazarus, that was not true. Anytime, day or night, we were welcome there."

"All thirteen of you?"

"All of us, including the women that serve the master. Anytime."

Nearing Bethany, the followers stopped beneath a grove of trees outside the village. Jesus lifted his hand. "We will rest here." He turned to the servant who accompanied them from the Jordan. "Go tell Martha and Mary we have come."

The servant hurried toward the village.

The followers were resting in the shade of the large trees when Martha rushed up and hugged Jesus. She sobbed, "If you had been here my brother would not have died."

Jesus tenderly wiped a tear from her cheek. "Your brother will rise again."

Martha sniffed. "I know he will rise again at the resurrection ... at the last day."

Jesus took her face in his hands. "I am the resurrection and the life ..." His next words were spoken softly and Nicodemus couldn't make them out, but several of the apostles standing close bent to listen.

Nicodemus saw Martha nod her head before she turned and hurried back toward town.

Within minutes, Mary rushed to Jesus. She fell at his feet sobbing. Her words repeated Martha's—"If you had been here he wouldn't have died."

Jesus turned to the others who had come with Mary. His voice choked. "Where have you laid him?"

One old man beckoned. "Come and see."

They followed him to a bluff near the grove of trees. The smooth rock was topped with vines and the face of the stone had been hollowed for many graves. Some were already overgrown with vines, but one was new.

Jesus stopped, facing the disc-shaped rock covering the tomb. A large crowd had followed Mary and they crowded the Master. He stood in silence. The crowd hushed. Tears streamed down his face. He took a deep breath and his voice echoed off the barren rocks. "Roll the stone away."

Martha, standing nearby, looked startled. "But Lord, he has been dead four days now. The body will stink."

Jesus wiped away tears and raised his hand, his voice firm. "Remove it."

Several of the men looked at one another, then back at Jesus. They cautiously approached the stone. Glancing back once more, they threw their strength into the task. The stone grated in its channel. The men backed into the semi-circle of people and stared into the gaping blackness.

The voice of Jesus thundered, "Lazarus, come forth."

No one moved. Nicodemus shuddered. He stood gazing into the depths of the tomb. Then ... something moved. Slowly, a draped figure appeared in the blackness. Nicodemus felt a chill creep up his spine.

A gasp went through the crowd, and a tall, shrouded figure emerged. A woman screamed and dropped to her knees. Another cried, "It's him, Lazarus has risen!"

Jesus ordered, "Remove the grave clothes from him."

Stunned silence was followed by murmurs, then shouts. Half the crowd dropped to their knees. Others shouted, "Hosanna, Praise God!"

Jesus commanded, "Let him go."

Mary and Martha rushed to Lazarus and unwound the grave clothes.

Nicodemus, trembling, looked around. Several members of the Sanhedrin were in the throng that had witnessed the resurrection. In back, he thought he recognized the fat figure as Ahaz.

Sure enough, Ahaz whined, "He's alive. The dead one is alive!" He turned and rushed as fast as his plump figure would move, to the road leading to Jerusalem.

Lazarus' face was pale, but his smile was radiant as both sisters held him in their arms and wept.

* * *

It was late when Nicodemus arrived at his home. Deborah, embracing him, was quick to sense his turmoil. "You are troubled, my husband, what has happened? Was your time on the Jordan unpleasant?"

Nicodemus slumped into a chair. "Please call Mother. I want to talk to both of you."

The look on his face caused Deborah to frown. She walked into the adjoining room to call Muriel.

The two women sat in stillness as Nicodemus recounted his trip and told of the events in Bethany. "Lazarus had been in that tomb for four days, and at Jesus' voice, he came out. He talked to us, he ate with us ... He is alive, it can be no mistake."

Muriel, her eyes wide, spoke. "It is a great miracle, but if we proclaim him as the Messiah—" She dropped her head into her hands. Sobs shook her body.

Deborah straightened her gown. "If it becomes known that we are believers in Him ..." She tucked her lower lip between her teeth.

"We cannot deny this power any longer." She sat straight. "Please, Husband, go slow. I am not ready to reject all my father and your father have believed since our birth. If we accept this one ... The Sanhedrin has decreed that anyone confessing him to be the Messiah will be cast out of their synagogue. We must be sure before—before we leave everything we stand for."

Nicodemus hadn't reached a point of decision, but his wife was right. What was he to do? Passover would begin in one week and the full Sanhedrin would assemble at the beginning of the Feast.

*   *   *

Across the city, Caiaphas was meeting with his father-in-law and his inner circle of Council members.

Ahaz gestured wildly. "But I tell you, Caiaphas, this was no trick. He was in that tomb for four days; many there had handled his dead body. He rose from the dead."

Another priest affirmed, "This Jesus has the power, the power of the Almighty."

Annas growled, "Or the power of Beelzebub."

A Sadducee whispered, "We will have to kill Lazarus, too. He's living proof of the power of this false messiah.

At his comment, several shouted, and it took Caiaphas some time to regain control. A strange chill filled the chamber. Caiaphas rose. There was a deadly silence. A strange solemnity covered his face. "You are all foolish," he prophesied. "Do you not realize that it is better for one man to die, than our whole nation perish?"

The Council sat in silence, then without a word, one by one, filed into the temple square. The last to leave was Ahaz, trembling all over.

*   *   *

Two days after Lazarus' awakening, a band of believers assembled at his home in Bethany. Nicodemus was invited, as was Deborah. During the festivities, Mary stood behind Jesus and held the alabaster cruse Joanna had brought her. She tugged at the sealed lid and the soft stone broke. The ointment gushed onto Jesus' feet. The scent filled the room and Mary bent and wiped the Nazarene's feet with her hair.

One disciple, Judas Iscariot, mumbled, "What a waste. This perfume could have been sold and the money given to the poor."

Jesus turned and glared at Judas. "Leave her alone. This was intended for the day of my burial. You have the poor with you always, but you will not always have me."

Judas glanced around the room. He clenched his teeth, rose and hurried out.

Chapter Eighteen

Last Week

Joseph stretched his arms to the sky. Both he and Nicodemus breathed the fresh morning air. From their position on the temple wall, they looked across to the Mount of Olives. Joseph said, "This is the day that the Lord has made."

Nicodemus had to admit it was a beautiful day, but he hadn't slept much last night. They watched the people streaming into the city. The temple was crowded more than usual this Passover. This week it was his duty to serve in the temple, an honor he received only twice a year. This time, it occurred during Passover week. He caught strange sounds coming from the top of the hill across the valley. In the distance, he heard something. He turned to his cousin, his face puzzled.

Joseph's eyebrows lifted. "Sounds like chanting or yelling ..."

"A little of both. Look." Nicodemus pointed to the road that snaked down the Kidron Valley. "That throng of people ... some are putting palm branches and their cloaks on the roadway."

They watched as the mass of people descended into the Kidron Valley. One rode on a donkey. A throng of children chased him, waving fronds and chanting. The words "Hosanna" and "Blessed is the King of Israel" echoed across the valley. The figure on the donkey lifted his arms to the growing crowd.

Joseph cried, "It's the Nazarene. That's Jesus riding the donkey. Those men following him are his apostles. Look, right beside him ... those are the sons of Zebedee."

Several Sanhedrin members joined Nicodemus and Joseph on the platform to watch. Ahaz gasped. "Look at that crowd, and the Nazarene's leading them. The whole world is going out to him! Hundreds are following him." He turned and rumbled down the steps, his short legs almost giving way as he hit the bottom.

Joseph snickered. "He's headed back to the council room. Caiaphas and Annas will be well informed of the arrival of the Nazarene."

By this time, the procession had reached the brook and headed up the hill toward the Beautiful Gate. Other people had formed a corridor. The cheering grew louder. The children were dancing and waving their palm branches jubilantly. Their singing had become a recurring chant. "Hallelujah! Hosanna! Blessed is he who comes in the name of the Lord!"

Nicodemus touched Joseph's arm. "We'd better get to the Council meeting. If we were wondering where the Nazarene was, now we know." Before Nicodemus and Joseph reached the temple court, the first of the shouting children entered the gates. Their palm branches moved like a wind-blown forest. Their chant dominated the sounds of the busy temple court.

From the far side, Ahaz, his big body bouncing to a blocking position, shouted, "Command these children to be quiet! This is the temple of God!"

A voice cut above the din—it was Jesus. "If they remain silent, even the stones will cry out." Jesus alighted from the donkey and stood facing the red-faced Pharisee.

Ahaz stood, mouth wide, speechless. Jesus turned, his finger pointed to the money-changers and merchants selling animals for sacrifice. "Get these things out of here. This is a house of prayer!"

There was a sudden flurry among the merchants, and the money-changers scooped their neat stacks of coins into bags.

Jesus, his eyes flashing, took a step toward the stalls.

Joseph nudged Nicodemus. "This is just like the last time he cleared the temple. Those sellers aren't about to face another confrontation."

Within minutes, the bawling cattle, fluttering birds, and tables of coins were gone. From the north court, a procession marched forward.

Caiaphas, his ornate headpiece reflecting in the sun, strode toward the Nazarene. Caiaphas demanded, "Tell us, by what authority are you doing these things?" His fists were tight balls. "And who gave you this authority?"

The crowd quieted as Jesus paused, then replied, "I will also ask you a question." He took a step toward the high priest. "The baptism of John, was it from heaven or from men?"

Caiaphas' mouth moved silently and Annas whispered in his ear. The crowd grew quiet watching the encounter. Caiaphas turned, and without a word marched toward his chambers.

Walking by Joseph, Nicodemus grumbled, "We have Sanhedrin business, let's get to our meeting."

Nicodemus and Joseph were some of the last to join the Council. The members were in several huddles debating loudly. Bava shouted, "This man is trying to destroy our God-given authority!" Another yelled, "I tell you, I was there, Lazarus was dead, he was in the tomb for four days, I saw him." Joseph shook his head as they made their way to their usual places in the chamber.

Caiaphas almost broke his staff as he banged it on the floor for order. "Take your seats! Sit down! This session will come to order!" He was panting before everything quieted. He sat, clearing his throat. "We have all seen what this false prophet has done, even in our holy temple. There is no shame or humility in this man."

From the far side of the chamber, a young member named Saul rose. He had never spoken before. Everyone turned to look at him. "I say he must die for claiming to be sent from God."

One of the Pharisees yelled, "Saul is right!" Another shouted, "How often is one raised from the dead? I was there, I saw it." It seemed everyone had an opinion.

Caiaphas smashed his staff to the floor. "There will be silence!" He smiled approval to the young man. "As Saul of Tarsus has perceived, and so have some of us determined, this usurper must die." Another murmur went through the Council. "We must be cautious. The mob thinks he is the very power of God, and they will riot at his bidding. We don't want the Romans swooping down to slaughter us all. We need to find a time when he is alone, then we can take him."

Joseph stood.

Caiaphas looked surprised. He didn't acknowledge Joseph, yet all the Council turned to stare at the man from Arimathea, one who seldom spoke.

"Fellow members of the Council, in the past days we have proclaimed that anyone who admits to being one of his disciples should be removed from his synagogue and any member of the Sanhedrin be expelled. We have done these things in fear and without considering whether this unknown miracle worker has done acts only God himself could perform."

Caiaphas stood, his face livid with rage. "I do not—!"

Joseph's voice boomed. "We have done these things without considering whether this man—" He looked around the chamber and stared from face to face. "Whether this unknown man from Nazareth could really be the Messiah we have hoped and prayed for."

The members of chamber sat stunned until Annas stumbled to his feet. "This is blasphemy!" His words were amplified by others who stood, waving their fists. Their cries filled the chamber, but they didn't seem to frighten Joseph. When he had said his piece, he walked out.

Nicodemus sat in shock. His body quivered as he watched his best friend stride from the room. He wanted to join him but his feet wouldn't move. He felt hot tears flowing down his cheeks. Why didn't he speak? At that moment he despised his cowardliness.

* * *

That evening, Nicodemus stood staring at the darkening sky. He hardly heard Deborah as she entered their sleeping quarters. "You didn't eat anything at our evening meal. Something is wrong. Tell me." She put her arm around his neck and stood staring at the early stars.

He leaned his head on hers. Except for his breath, there was silence.

She dropped to her knees before him and he knelt with her, the light of the oil lamp showing the concern in her face. "My husband, if we are indeed one flesh then I need to know."

Nicodemus told his account of the day. He finished with a moan. "Who is this Jesus? Joseph believes in him, I have seen enough to believe, yet ..." He caught his breath and held her hands so tightly that she winced in pain.

"My husband, you are a good man. This I know. You must search your heart, and then follow it. I've never heard this Jesus; I've only seen him from a distance." Her eyes searched his face. "Be assured, because of you, I too, am wondering if this man of Galilee is the Messiah. Is this the one my father has sought and prayed for? Tomorrow I will be in the temple courts to hear him. If it means we become outcasts, like ... I am afraid your cousin has become, so be it."

Nicodemus watched her as she turned to go. God indeed had sent a help-meet into his life.

*   *   *

The busiest day of Passover was the second day. Joanna pushed her way through the crowds in the temple. With Jesus present in Jerusalem, the crowd was chattering with excitement. She spotted several of his followers and made her way toward them. She waved to the sons of Zebedee, then she saw a face she never expected to see. "Deborah, what are you doing here?" She gave her sister-in-law a hug.

Deborah blushed. "I just had to come. I had to hear him."

Joanna put her hand under Deborah's chin. "You've been crying?" She held her at arm's length, eyes searching.

Deborah frowned. "My husband is troubled. I had to see this teacher for myself."

Joanna took her sister-in-law's hand. "Come, He's here somewhere." She pulled her toward a knot of disciples. "Over there." She pointed.

Deborah stopped, puzzled. "That plain looking one, near the wall of the temple?" She shook her head. "He doesn't look like a prophet."

Joanna chuckled. "Come, you'll see. Don't be surprised when you meet him. He says things you'd never anticipate, but you'll see." She dragged Deborah through the crowd.

Approaching Jesus, Joanna stretched her hand. "Teacher, I have brought one who wants to meet you."

Jesus looked deeply into Deborah's eyes. "Ah, the wife of Nicodemus. Your husband is a man of deep thought, and a good heart."

Deborah's mouth dropped open in surprise. "You know who I am?" Her eyebrows knit together. "How do you know me?"

Jesus touched her hand. "You have come to find out if I have been sent from God. Then stay. Let your heart listen."

They were near the treasury, where a waist-high carved box was guarded by two temple soldiers. Two priests moved people into a line in front of it. The file shuffled forward and one by one they dropped offerings into the treasury. The sound of trumpets echoed across the courtyard. The temple guards snapped to rigid attention and the priests tending the crowd made an opening in the line. A procession of ornately dressed priests marched toward the coffer.

Annas and Caiaphas led the solemn procession, dressed in silken robes of blue with tall priestly hats. Caiaphas wore the sacred breastpiece with its twelve various colored stones shimmering in the light. The congregation moved back to watch the dual line of the leading Jews make their Passover offerings.

Jesus turned and joined the onlookers as, one by one, the priests and the leaders dropped their gifts into the treasury. Several poured in bags of coins, and the stream of silver flashed and jingled as it fell.

One man lifted his gift high in the morning sun and a jewel sparkled in the light. He sighed, and then dropped it into the box.

Someone far back in the long column accidentally dropped his coins. The crowd twittered as he crawled to gather them. During the break in the line, a bent woman in tattered garments slipped forward and quickly dropped her coins into the treasury and moved to the side.

Jesus strode forward, his voice filling the court. "Do you see this woman?"

The old woman cringed as Jesus' arm enveloped her frail figure. With horror and embarrassment, she looked around, her lips trembling.

Jesus lifted his palm. "This poor widow has given more than all the others."

Caiaphas and Annas stared in wide-eyed amazement.

Jesus lifted his arm toward the priests. "All these people gave their gifts out of their wealth; but she, out of her poverty, put in all she had to live on."

Caiaphas turned red and clenched his teeth, then turned and led his followers back to their chambers.

The small woman looked around and squeezed Jesus' arm. A hint of a smile creased her face as she disappeared into the crowd.

Joanna turned to Deborah. "Please stay. I want you to watch and listen to him. He does not dress like a king, but he talks of a new kind of kingdom." They sat amid the disciples and listened.

*   *   *

Late that evening, a priest rushed into the small chamber of the high priest. A man followed him, covering his face. The priest told

Caiaphas, "I have found a man who will lead us to him. He requires thirty pieces of silver for this service."

Caiaphas leaned forward. "How do I know that this man can find him? He has escaped our previous attempts."

The hooded figure moved forward. "I can take you to him." He threw back the hood. "I am one of his apostles. I know the place he goes to pray. My name is Judas, called Iscariot."

Caiaphas studied him, and then summoned his servant. "Get thirty pieces of silver and bring them to me." He turned to Judas, how will you point him out to us?"

Judas bent forward, his voice soft. "The one I kiss will be the Nazarene."

*   *   *

From his window, Joseph watched the people descending the stairs from the temple. He rested from his reading.

A man from Arimathea entered and bowed. "Joseph, your father, Joram, is very sick. He bids you join him at once. Please come with me. He may not last long."

Joseph rose and clutched the servant's arm. Frowning, he said, "I was preparing for the whole family to come for the Feast. Everything is prepared. The furniture is all in place—He sighed, and then dropped his hands. "I'll come."

Joseph told Rachel, "I must be at my father's side in his sickness. Will you and the children go with me, or stay here in Jerusalem?" He added, "I am sure you would be welcome in Nicodemus' home for the feast."

Rachel took off her apron and straightened her dress. "The children and I will go, but it will take some time to get them ready.

Will you ready the donkey? It is a hard trip for our little ones." She sighed. "We have made such preparations, for nothing."

Joseph called over his shoulder, "I will go ahead and our servant will accompany you." He paused, then suggested, "Perhaps someone else will have need of our upper room."

Chapter Nineteen

The Long Night

The Jews milling around the temple stairways were in their best Passover clothes. Two women pushed through the festive sojourners toward a quiet spot behind the bustling market. Deborah was wearing her best blue gown with a scarf of dark blue. Joanna wore her gown of gray, proclaiming her widowhood. She knew her dress was appropriate, but couldn't wait to marry Chuza next spring and change her drab colors to those of a bride.

Joanna pulled her sister-in-law across the uneven cobblestones. They found a bench with a good view of the temple glistening in the morning sun. "Over here, Deborah, this is one of my favorite spots to watch the people." She gave Deborah a hug. "I'm glad you decided to come with me today, with Nicodemus on Temple duty. It gives us a chance to talk."

Deborah loosened her scarf and took Joanna's arm. "It's quite warm for this early in the morning." She leaned toward Joanna. "Are you sure he will be here, at the temple?"

"Jesus has been here every day during this feast. I am confident he will appear. Are you ready to see him again?" She felt Deborah's hand tighten on her arm.

Deborah brushed a strand of loose hair. "My husband is becoming a believer. I need to hear this Nazarene again. I just don't know. Tell me, why do you believe this is the one we have waited for?"

Joanna started to answer, but glancing across the open space, rose and waved to a man carrying an armful of food. "John! John, over here!"

The man turned, waved, and strode toward the two women. Both rose to greet him. Deborah cocked her head, her eyebrows raised. "Are you John from the Galilee? My husband has spoken of you."

Joanna said, "John, this is the wife of Nicodemus, her name is Deborah. She is my sister-in-law and she is seeking answers." She turned. "And yes, this is John, one of the apostles from Galilee."

John placed his load aside and the three sat on the wide bench beside the wall. He studied Deborah's face. "So you seek answers? The teacher is better at answering hard questions than I."

Joanna touched his hand. "She wants to talk to Jesus later, but John, tell her why you became a follower."

John blinked several times before answering. "Why do I believe? That's a long story. Perhaps someday I should write it down. I think my reason for belief is not the countless miracles I have seen him perform, even though when he calmed a raging sea and raised Lazarus from the tomb these confirmed my faith. He has great power, yet Jesus touched my heart as no one has ever done." He took a deep breath. "He is a complete man. He gets tired, he weeps, and he's moved to compassion. But, he is more than a man. It's very difficult to explain. I've asked myself why I believe many times." His eyes met hers. "You will need to talk to him yourself. Then you can judge."

Deborah asked, "Will he be in the temple today? I have many questions needing answers."

John said, "He will be here later. I must be going. I have to deliver this food to my Uncle Malcus." He lifted his load. "These are things Uncle needs for preparing the Passover meal. When in the city, I usually stay at his home."

Joanna asked, "Will you be with your uncle for the meal?"

John shook his head. "No, the master said he has a great desire to eat this Passover with us ..." John's face became troubled. " ... before he suffers."

John turned and vanished into the crowd. The women looked at one another. His last words sent a jolt of fear through them.

*   *   *

The sun had almost reached its pinnacle. The lower staircase leading to the Court of the Gentiles was full of people: disciples, onlookers, and most of the Sanhedrin. Jesus stood facing the crowd. He had just finished telling them a parable about some evil tenants who had, in a final act of greed, killed the son of their master. Even the unlearned understood the story was aimed at the leading Jews.

Caiaphas stood at the top of the staircase, surrounded by several Herodians. He shouted, "Tell us, teacher, is it lawful to pay taxes to Caesar or not?"

Jesus stared at the crowd. "Show me a denarius.". Whose portrait and inscription are on it?"

There was hurried confusion to find a coin, and then one was passed to him. He handed it to a priest standing near.

"Whose portrait and inscription are on it?"

The priest glanced at it. "Caesar's image."

Jesus pointed to the temple, his voice echoing from the walls. "Then, render unto Caesar what is Caesar's, and unto God what is God's."

The crowd chuckled. Deborah heard a familiar bass voice say "Amen!" She turned and saw her father, Gamaliel, standing several steps above.

Caiaphas and his friends whispered to one another.

A Sadducee stood. "Teacher, Moses wrote that if a man's brother leaves a wife, but no children, the brother must marry the widow and have children for his brother."

Jesus nodded.

"Now there were seven brothers, the first one died and left the woman childless. The second, then the third married her. Eventually all seven married her and died, leaving her childless. Finally, the woman died too. Now, Teacher, at the resurrection, whose wife shall she be?"

Jesus' gaze swept the crowd. "The people of this generation marry and are given in marriage. But those who are in the resurrection will neither marry or be given in marriage. They are like the angels."

Gamaliel shook his fist and proclaimed, "Well said, Teacher." Others murmured approval.

The band of Jews walked back to the temple grounds, grumbling as they went.

Jesus spoke to the multitude. "Beware the teachers of the law. They love to walk around in flowing robes and be greeted in the marketplace and have the important seats in the synagogues and places of honor at banquets." He frowned. "They devour widows' houses and for a show make lengthy prayers. Such men will be punished more severely."

Again, Deborah heard her father's loud amen. She almost laughed out loud.

* * *

Deborah and Muriel spread the white dinner cloth, one used three times a year. The ornate blue edging created a special effect for the Seder meal to come. The aroma of roasting lamb filled the room. Joanna carefully replaced each tallow candle in the menorah, while Nicodemus slid the hidden manna between the special napkins. He carefully placed the four silver cups before his chair. He paused, feeling a sting in his heart. They had no child to ask the traditional questions or search for the hidden manna. For this feast, his sister would act the part of the child. He breathed a silent prayer. "'Please, God, may we be blessed with a little one." He turned to watch his sister, amazed—she would never become a mother—yet, since she had become a follower of Jesus, her heart had found peace and contentment. He only wished his troubled soul knew that peace. He went to his room to prepare his mind for the Passover. Tomorrow would be his last day of temple duty for four months, but tonight he would enjoy this sacred meal.

As the tallow candles burned low, with gray-haired Joanna playing the part of the inquiring child, Nicodemus repeated the ceremonial story, telling the true meaning of the Passover and Israel's exodus from captivity.

Nicodemus finished the ceremonial blessing. He caught himself wondering how many homes in the city were celebrating this same ritual. He watched as Deborah blew out the candles and replaced the special cups and menorah. He hoped for a good night's rest, but this was a troubling time. He almost caressed Deborah, but stiffened—

he was to remain without the joys of his wife during his time of purification.

* * *

Nicodemus awoke to hear a soft but persistent tapping at the door. Deborah was up before he was fully awake. He heard her utter a surprised, "John, is that you? It's still dark."

Nicodemus was tying on his robe as he entered the main room. "John, what's happened, where are the others?"

John sat on the cushioned chair, breathing hard and shivering. Deborah brought a blanket and wrapped it around his shoulders.

Joanna entered the room. She rushed to his side and put an arm around him. "You're alone. Where are the other apostles? Where is—?" Her words froze on her lips.

"They have taken him. We were in the garden. They bound him and took him to Annas." John's head dropped into his hands, he sobbed.

Nicodemus raised his voice. "Wait, wait, didn't you all have the Passover together?"

Deborah added wood to the coals and blew them to life. She put a brass kettle on the hook. "You're shivering, John. Just a few minutes and you will have something warm to drink. Tell us what happened, please. Start from the beginning. Tell us everything."

John took a deep breath, and shook his head. His eyes were tired and bloodshot. "Our Passover Feast was one Jesus said he longed to eat with us. It was splendidly prepared for us. I understand that the upper room belonged to your cousin."

"Joseph?"

John smiled weakly. He sighed. "We were all at one big table." "Just as we were about to begin, the teacher took off his outer garment and tied a towel around his waist. Then, to our surprise, he washed each of our feet."

Joanna blurted, "Jesus washed your feet?"

John chin dropped. "Peter, always the one to speak, told the Lord to never wash his."

Deborah handed a steaming cup of tea to John.

"Jesus said if he didn't wash his feet they were finished."

Muriel, joining the three, asked softly, "What did Peter do?"

"He changed his words quickly. After Jesus took off the towel, he asked us if we knew what he had done. He said unless we wash each other's feet and become one another's servants, we would not be his disciples. He also said Peter would deny him three times before the cock crowed."

All four listeners sat quietly and John continued. "At the supper, Jesus said one of us would betray him. We were stunned. All the way around the table each asked, 'Is it me Lord?' Then Jesus did something we didn't understand at the time, he gave a piece of bread to Judas. It was a sign that he was the betrayer. He told Judas—"

Joanna interrupted. "Judas Iscariot?"

"Yes, Iscariot. He told him to go and do what he must. And Judas got up and left."

Joanna tilted her head. "Then ...?"

John sipped his drink. "He told us more of his coming trials. He prayed for all of us. Then we walked to the Garden of Gethsemane where he frequently goes."

Joanna said, "I've gone there with him. That's where he goes to pray."

"It was late; all was dark except for the stars ... it was cold. Jesus took Peter, James and me further into the garden to pray with him. It was so late ... I tried to stay awake, but ... I fell asleep. Later, he awakened us. His face was covered with sweat. He told us to pray so we would not fall into temptation." John drained the cup and set it on the floor. His eyes were teary. "The third time he awakened us, he told us to get up. His betrayer had come."

Nicodemus asked, "Betrayer?"

John's words were choked. "As I stood, I saw the lights coming through the trees, many torches and lanterns. Leading the mob was Judas, followed by scores of soldiers."

Joanna frowned. "Roman soldiers?"

John shook his head. "No, they were not Romans, they were the temple soldiers and my Uncle Malcus was with them. When they first came, Jesus said, 'Who do you seek?' and someone said 'Jesus.' He replied, 'I am he.' When he said that, they all fell back. Jesus demanded, 'I am the one you seek, let these others go.' Some of the other apostles ran off, but Peter took his sword to defend Jesus. He swung—I think at Judas—but it struck Malcus on the ear and sliced it, so it was hanging loose. Jesus told Peter to put up his sword. He reached up and restored Malcus' ear."

Deborah blurted, "He did what?"

"His ear was almost off. Jesus healed him." John's fingers touched his own ear. "My uncle just stood there. There was no blood, nothing." He placed his palms together. "They bound Jesus and led him away." His voice choked. "I heard one say they were taking him to Annas' home for trial, and I followed them along with Peter."

Nicodemus stood. "According to our law, it is unlawful to try one by night."

"It was the third watch of the night. My cousin is the chief steward and I had often been to the home of Annas. There is an iron gate to close it from the street. It has a courtyard before the house. Since those guarding the gate knew me, I was permitted to enter. Peter, they kept on the street. Later, I asked the guard to let Peter into the outer court. I entered the house and listened to Annas and the other members of the council as they tried to trap Jesus. Several accused him, but their testimonies didn't agree."

Nicodemus paced. "Those Sadducees stop at nothing."

"Ahaz and several other Pharisees were there too."

Nicodemus smacked his fist into his palm. "This is against our law!"

"After a long time, Annas decided Jesus should be taken across town to Caiaphas' home. Peter was standing, warming by the fire, and just as they were taking him out, one of the guards pointed at Peter. 'You are a Galilean, your speech gives you away.' Peter shouted a curse at the soldier and yelled, 'I don't even know him!' Just then, from beyond the walls, a rooster crowed. This was just as Jesus was led from the inner court, his eyes met Peter's. Peter's hands covered his face, and he ran into the street, sobbing. I had never seen him cry before."

The little group sat around John as he dropped his head into his hands. "I just came here. I didn't know where else it would be safe. They are watching the home of Lazarus, and Judas knows where Joseph's home is. May I rest here for a little while?"

Joanna put her arms around him and led him to a pallet across the room.

Nicodemus went back to bed and tried to force his mind to cease, at least for a few hours of rest before his service at the temple began.

*   *   *

The sky was beginning to lighten as Deborah nudged Nicodemus. "My husband, someone is tapping at the door. Do you want to go, or should I answer it?"

Nicodemus was still half asleep as he squinted at the dim light of morning. He threw on a robe and shuffled to the door. "Who is it?"

A whisper came. "It's Joseph."

Nicodemus jolted wide awake, jerked the door open. "I thought you were in Arimathea with your father."

Joseph put his finger to his lips. "Tell your family my father is paralyzed and can't speak, but he's resting well. I have come to Jerusalem at the command of Pontius Pilate. The Jews have arrested Jesus and they are planning to bring him to trial."

Nicodemus was wide awake now. "John brought us the news of his arrest early this morning, but when are they putting him on trial?" He paused. "How did you get here so quickly?"

"Pilate sent a centurion with an extra horse; we rode fast." Joseph's voice rose. "They will bring Jesus to trial at the Praetorium. You must assemble those of the Sanhedrin who are not in Caiaphas' bunch. We must stop this thing!"

Nicodemus shook his head. "I'm on temple duty, but Joanna will try to reach the disciples. Deborah can tell her father of the trial, and he can try to assemble the priests. We will try. Will you come in?"

"No, I told the centurion I would be there. He barely gave me leave to see you. I must meet with the governor within the hour. Tell the disciples. We must spread the word now."

Chapter Twenty

Friday

Joseph, accompanied by the centurion, climbed the four steps to the Praetorium. Standing by the polished marble columns were four Roman guards, two on each side. The governor's banners fluttered in the morning breeze. Ominously propped against the far wall was a line of crosses—the silent threat of Roman justice. The centurion entered the inner courtyard and motioned for Joseph to wait. "I will tell the governor you have arrived." He strode through the garden and into the main palace.

Watching the servants scurrying about the court, Joseph could feel the tension. Pontius Pilate, in his best armor, met him, his voice agitated. "These cursed Jews have arrested this Nazarene and insist on bringing him to trial today." His brow wrinkled and his words spewed contempt. "I don't understand your wretched people."

"It is a time of special celebration for the Jewish people."

"This is what they do to celebrate? Holy Zeus! They want me to kill a person so they can celebrate?"

Joseph stood silent. He had no answer.

Pilate commanded a servant, "Get the royal chair and put it right here." He turned back to Joseph. "I want you standing behind me on the left. If there is any question of the Jewish law or customs, I need you beside me, understand?" He turned to another officer. "When Caiaphas and his cohorts arrive, summon my entrance."

He turned to Joseph and motioned to follow him inside. He plopped into a chair. "Tell me, Jew, why does your Council bring one of your own to me for trial?"

Joseph felt the conflict raging in his own heart. He didn't want to explain to outsiders his belief in Jesus, or defend the Jewish high court. "Our Council doesn't have the authority to execute anyone, only Rome has that authority, or so I'm told."

Pilate frowned at Joseph, but just then the centurion came in and saluted. "Your Excellence, the priests are assembling in the courtyard. Also, they have a large crowd with them." Pilate sat staring at the wall for a long time. Finally, he exhaled and stood erect. He led Joseph and his chosen soldiers to the judgment seat.

Caiaphas, in his priestly garments, followed by Annas and four other Sanhedrin members, led a cordon of temple soldiers. They surrounded the bound Jesus and led him to the platform.

Joseph looked at the assembled crowd. Outside of a score of priests, the mob was the street rabble of the city. A few standing along the back wall were Zealots and Herodians.

Pilate pulled his golden robe aside and seated himself. "What charges are you bringing against this man?"

"If he were not a criminal, we would not turn him over to you," Caiaphas answered.

Pilate sneered. "Then take him and judge him by your own law."

Annas said, "We have no right to execute anyone. He claims to be a king."

Pilate rose and motioned for the guards to bring Jesus into the inner palace. Joseph followed, placing himself behind Pilate's left shoulder as instructed. Once inside, Pilate faced the Nazarene. "Are you then the king of the Jews?"

"Is this your own idea?" Jesus replied calmly, "Or did others tell you about me?"

"Am I a Jew? It was your people who brought you to me. What is it you have done?" He moved within arm's length. "What is all this kingdom talk I hear?"

"My kingdom is not of this world, if it were, my servants would fight. My kingdom is from another place."

Pilate looked confused. "You are a king then?"

Jesus nodded. "You are right in saying I am a king. For this cause I came to this world, to testify to the truth."

Pilate sighed. "What is truth?" The question hung in the air. He turned and led the squad back to the judgment seat. His voice rang from the walls. "I find no charge against him."

The murmur from the crowd rose as Jesus reappeared. Someone yelled, "Death to the Galilean!"

Pilate's eyes became slits. His right fist slapped into his palm. "That's right, he is from Galilee." He tapped his finger. "Jew, I understand Herod is in the city for the Passover, is this true?"

"That is what I've heard."

Pilate turned to his centurion. "Take this Jesus to Herod. I will let the king of Galilee judge one of his own."

Four soldiers pulled Jesus through the crowd. As he passed, some spit on him, others derided him. Joseph cringed as the soldiers jerked Jesus through the mob.

Pilate looked pleased as he led his servants back into the palace. He muttered to Joseph, "Herod, I've heard, has wanted to see this healer. We'll let him decide his fate."

* * *

An hour later, the centurion returned, Jesus still bound. He stood quietly before Pilate. The centurion reported, "Your Excellency, Herod questioned our prisoner for a long time. The Nazarene didn't say a word. I think Herod wanted to see some miracle. He gave no decision."

The crowd outside was chanting, "Crucify! Crucify!" Pilate sat in his inner chamber brooding. Just when he was about to rise, one of Pilate's servants handed him a note. Joseph watched Pilate's eyes go wide, fear spreading across his face. He turned to Joseph, his voice a whisper, "Jew, my wife had a vision telling her I was not to have anything to do with this ... this righteous man." Pilate turned to Jesus. "Who are you?"

Without waiting for an answer, Pilate commanded the centurion, "I want this Nazarene scourged." Turning to Joseph again, he demanded, "What do these cursed Jews want anyway?"

Joseph shook his head. "Outside of the priests, most of this crowd is just the rabble of the streets. The men standing in back are Herodians and several call themselves Zealots."

Pilate turned to his servant. "I want you to fashion a crown of thorns—use those big ones from the rock wall. Take the old red drape that covered the back hall and make him a robe. We'll give them a king! Maybe then they'll show some pity."

The soldiers yanked Jesus by the rope around his neck into the adjoining hall. Joseph heard the beating. He cringed as the lash struck again and again. What seemed an eternity later, he heard the soldiers mocking, with shouts of "Hail, king of the Jews!"

It was almost mid-day when the Roman soldiers returned, dragging the bleeding body of Jesus. He wore a faded red cape, blood dripping from the thorns pressed into his head. Joseph's stomach lurched as he looked at the beaten body. Jesus was held erect by two soldiers. Pilate rose and led Jesus and the others to the judgment place.

The crowd gasped as the battered prisoner was dragged to the platform. After a moment of silence, Pilate shouted, "Behold, the man!" Many looked both sickened and startled, then the murmur began.

Pilate raised his hands for silence. He yelled, "By custom, at Passover, I release to you one prisoner. Shall I release Barabbas or this Nazarene?"

A single voice rose from the back. "Release Barabbas! Barabbas!" The chant repeated and increased. "Barabbas! Release Barabbas!"

Pilate frowned and raised his fists. "Then what shall I do with this, your king?"

From a priest came a guttural voice. "Crucify him." The chant grew and soon the walls drummed, "Crucify! Crucify!"

Pilate turned to Joseph. Joseph stood mute, too troubled to speak. Pilate pleaded, "Barabbas is a thief and murderer, and they know that. Do they hate this Nazarene so much they would release scum in his place? You Jews are strange." He turned to a nearby servant. "Go, get me a basin of water."

Caiaphas quieted the mob. "We have a law, and because of this law this infidel must die, for he claimed to be the son of God."

Pilate's mouth fell open. He stood and leaned toward Jesus, his eyes frantic. "Where do you come from?"

Jesus was silent.

"Don't you realize I have power to release or crucify you?"

Jesus voice, though weak, was calm. "You would have no power over me if it were not given to you from above. Therefore, the one who handed me over to you is guilty of a greater sin."

Pilate took the basin and sat down with it on his lap. The servant poured water over his hands and the governor proclaimed to the crowd, "This day I wash my hands of this man. I find no guilt in him. His blood will be on your hands."

A cold chill gripped Joseph. It raced up his spine as one of his fellow Sanhedrin members shouted, "His blood be on us and our children!"

Silence dropped over the courtyard. Pilate's arm was trembling as he turned to the centurion. "Crucify him."

Soldiers removed the red robe from Jesus while three others dragged one of the crosses toward the platform. Pilate rose and ordered, "Take those two thieves we captured with Barabbas and crucify them beside this ... this king of the Jews."

The centurion saluted Pilate and pulled his prisoner toward the gate. A soldier steadied Jesus as the centurion took Jesus' own robe and placed it on his bleeding shoulder. Two other soldiers lifted the cross to his back.

Chapter Twenty-One

The Cross

Joanna held Mary Magdalene's arm as they joined the mob following the procession. Just ahead of them was Jesus' mother and three other women. Ahead, the cordon of soldiers shoved the crowds aside to let the cross-laden Jesus drag his heavy burden through the winding streets. Joanna wiped the tears from her face and tried to hold the sobbing Mary upright. She didn't feel strong, but she knew her only chance to comfort Jesus was if she was there—as close as possible.

Jesus, bleeding from the beating and thorns piercing his scalp, stumbled. A black man standing near the procession caught the heavy crossbeam to keep it from falling on him. The centurion commanded the man to help Jesus bear the cross. With only a moment's hesitation, he strained and lifted the timber to his own shoulder.

Jesus turned to the weeping women. His voice weakly implored, "Daughters of Jerusalem, do not weep for me, but weep for your children." He grimaced as he lifted the lower end of the beam.

The procession moved forward. A soldier in the rear used his spear to prod the two other condemned men. "Move!"

In what seemed an eternity to Joanna, they wove through the crowded streets. Finally, reaching the low barren rock rising to the north of the city, they prepared for the crucifixion. The soldiers pushed the black man, named Simon of Cyrene, and Jesus aside, then dragged the cross to a flat place where a series of holes was cut in the rock. They stripped the prisoners of their garments and left only loin cloths. Jesus was pulled to the center cross. One soldier placed his feet on either side at the bottom of the beam, while another grasped his ankles. A soldier on either side grabbed a wrist and pulled him backward onto the crossbeam. He moaned as his raw back hit the rough wood.

A burly soldier, wearing a pocketed leather apron, knelt, his knee on Jesus' right arm. He took a nail the length of his hand, holding two more in his teeth. Finding the hollow spot of the wrist, he placed the point. He raised his heavy hammer.

The sound of the blow caused Joanna to cringe. A cry escaped her lips. The nail pierced Jesus' arm and buried itself in the wood. A second blow drove it deep into the cross. The soldier moved like a cat across the body and with two blows secured the left arm. Moving to the legs, he pulled the knees up, into a bent position, and placed the ankles together. He placed the last spike and, with two quick blows, impaled them both. He shuffled to the top of the cross and tacked a sign above Jesus' head.

The centurion lifted his arms and the three soldiers raised the cross to a vertical position. Then the cross thudded into the hole.

Joanna grabbed Jesus' mother to keep her from collapsing.

Jesus cried out, "Father, forgive them. They don't know what they are doing."

Mary Magdalene squinted at the sign above Jesus' head. "What does that say?"

Joanna puzzled at the three lines. "I can only read the last line. It says; 'Jesus of Nazareth, The King of the Jews."

Nearby, a priest was studying the same words. He walked to the centurion. "That sign should say, 'He said he was the King of the Jews.' It must be changed."

The centurion glared at him. "You want it changed? You see Pilate about it."

The thieves were nailed to the crosses on each side of Jesus. They screamed in pain until the weight of their bodies made it impossible for them to breathe. Their cries faded to strained moans.

John, the apostle, stood with the women. Joanna watched as Mary, Jesus' mother, crept to the foot of the cross. She studied the pain-convulsed face of her son. Both the apostle and Joanna moved beside her and put arms around her trembling figure. Mary's face was ashen and her lips shivered wordlessly. Her red eyes had run out of tears.

From the cross, Jesus said, "Dear woman, here is your son." Joanna looked up to see Jesus gaze rest on John.

John looked into his Lord's face. He nodded.

Jesus groaned again. Through clenched teeth, he whispered, "John, behold your mother."

John tightened his arm around Mary. "I will take care of her." He gulped.

It was after midday and the cloudless sky was bright above the hill. A small band of priests stood near the little huddle of followers. One yelled, "You saved others, now save yourself!" Another added, "Come down from the cross, and we'll believe you." Several others added their insults.

The four soldiers divided the garments of the dying men. The thief's garments were thrown aside as worthless. Jesus' garments had more value. After ripping the inner garment into four parts, one lifted Jesus' outer robe and growled, "This robe is seamless. Let's cast lots for it." He drew some markers from his pocket. All four dropped to their knees and began their game.

One thief taunted, "Aren't you the Christ? Save yourself and us." The thief on the other side cried, "Don't you fear God? We're here for our own sins; this one has done nothing wrong." He turned toward Jesus and pleaded, "Jesus, remember me when you come into your kingdom."

In the silence following, Jesus spoke to the second thief. "I tell you the truth, today you will be with me in paradise."

The fat priest Ahaz approached the foot of the cross. He mumbled incoherently. Several others had grown hoarse from their mocking. Only the weeping of the women filled the silence on the barren hill. The suffering men struggled to raise their bodies to a position where they gasped a few breaths before the pain in their ankles became overwhelming. This slow cycle of death by crucifixion, devised by the cruelty of Rome, was fearfully effective.

Jesus cried out, "I thirst!"

One of the soldiers dipped a sponge into a bucket at the foot of the cross and, with a long reed, lifted it to Jesus' lips. Jesus tasted it, then turned his head away and refused to drink.

Joanna wondered why he wouldn't drink if he was thirsty. John answered her wordless question. "They mix gall with vinegar. It's given to stop pain."

Joanna glanced upward. There were no clouds, but the sky was darkening.

The priests studied the dimming light and then looked at one another. As a group, they shuffled from the hill, leaving only the kneeling Ahaz. His eyes were wide as he stared up at the figure on the cross. His mouth moved, but nothing came out. Time crept slowly like a dark serpent relishing its prey—darkness increased.

The crowd was thinning as Jesus, looking into the growing darkness, cried, "My God, my God, why have you forsaken me?"

One in the crowd exclaimed, "He's calling Elijah!"

Another said, "Let's see if Elijah comes to rescue him."

The words were hardly spoken when the ground began to shake. Joanna moved beside Mary Magdalene. In the dim light the other followers clung to each other.

From the cross, Jesus said, "Father, into your hands, I commit my spirit."

Another stronger tremor shook the rock.

Jesus cried, "It is finished!"

At the foot of the cross, the centurion dropped to his knees. His whole body trembled. Joanna watched as his finger touched Jesus' foot.

The soldier turned away from the scene, tears trickled down his cheeks." Surely, this was the Son of God." A resounding crack filled the air and a split in the rock raced toward the city.

The last priest to leave knelt trembling in the darkness. He shook uncontrollably. Ahaz whimpered, "What have we done?"

Chapter Twenty-Two

Darkness

A centurion stood before Pontius Pilate. The governor was disturbed. "This Jesus—an innocent man—is crucified by my order, and yet this blasted Jewish Council is still unhappy. They want me to change my writing, do they?" He glared at the centurion. "Go to that self-righteous high-priest—tell him that what I have written is written!"

The centurion saluted and strode out.

Joseph, seated near the window, glanced at the dimming light.

The strain of the day showed on Pilate's face as he listened to the wails coming from the city streets.

Procula rushed into the room, her voice terrified. "My husband, I was in the garden and the sun is growing dark!"

"Clouds will—"

"There are no clouds!" Her voice was now a screech. "It's midday and getting dark! Look outside—see for yourself!"

Pilate clapped his hands. "Servants, bring lights." It was almost totally dark before a shaking servant brought several small lamps that cast flickering shadows across the chamber.

Procula shivered in the corner. "I told you to have nothing to do with this man, this Jesus." She turned to Joseph and wailed, "What

183

is it about this land? Does this God of yours even control the sun?"
She didn't wait for a reply but grabbed a lamp and rushed out.

From the dim light, Joseph watched fear creep across the governor's face.

* * *

In the temple across the city, Nicodemus finished his third sweeping of the polished cedar floor. He wondered, as he had so many times, if this holy place was any easier to clean back in the time of Solomon's temple. He only imagined what that gold-covered floor was like. This polished cedar floor was spotless, but gold?

He sighed, recalling the brutal history of this holy temple. He bitterly remembered the desecrations under Egyptians and Babylonians that had violated its sanctification. He cringed as he remembered the wicked kings of Israel who valued the gold more than God's holy place. This temple, built by Herod, was the most magnificent building in all of Israel, yet it paled in comparison to Solomon's temple. Herod provided gold to cover the frontal and the holy vessels. A gold interior for a place only seen by priests didn't match his ego.

Nicodemus gazed at the coals he had carefully stacked on the altar of incense. Their glow and that of the seven branched menorah were the only light in this windowless chamber. He always was reverent before this fire—*Shekinah*—the holy fire.

He walked to the small door used only by priests and into the adjoining storage room. He carefully filled a small censer with the sacred incense. His bare feet slid across the polished boards as he approached the blazing altar. He bowed before it, gently sprinkling the holy mixture on the coals. The aromatic smoke sizzled as it billowed toward the lofty ceiling. Smells of flower gardens and sweet balsam filled the air. The light of the giant candlestick cast flickering fingers on the walls as the gray smoke twisted and billowed toward the ceiling like a ghostly dancer.

He turned toward the heavy woven veil dividing the Holy Place and the Holy of Holies. Its crimson and blue design reached into the great darkness above. He had always been fascinated, watching this display of the mystic ballet of light and shadows on this curtain. He remembered his first time to witness this spectacle, so many Sabbaths ago.

He returned the censer to its spot and tried to concentrate on his priestly work. He had to keep from worrying about the events he feared were happening in the city around him. In the flickering smoke he imagined seeing a writhing figure on a pole above the fiery incense. He blinked, and the illusion faded.

Questions flooded into his mind. What was happening outside? Was the Nazarene on trial? Was the Roman governor hearing the case? Would other Pharisees be pleading on behalf of Jesus? In only a few hours, the sun would set and the Sabbath would begin—a most holy Sabbath, the Passover Sabbath.

He shook himself to the realities of his duty and walked to the table of showbread. He gathered the bread of the Presence and carried it to the preparation room. He broke the fresh bread carefully, one portion for each of the golden plates. He puzzled, as he always did, handling the heavy plates. Two were different, and their scratches testifying the truth of the tale. They were vessels of the original temple and had made the journey to Babylon and back, five centuries before.

When he reached the table, his fingers stroked the polished acacia wood. It was as silken as a baby's skin. He looked around the

Keith Ballard Farris

chamber. His preparation task was completed. The Holy Place was spotless: The candlestick was trimmed, the oil replenished, the altar of incense was ready and the table prepared. He knelt for prayers, hoping he would not be distracted by events happening outside this secluded chamber.

He had just begun to pray when he heard the priest's door creak. He turned to see Ahaz creep into the chamber. The fat priest carried a small torch.

Nicodemus demanded, "Ahaz, you know better than to bring strange fire into this place. Only the holy fire from the great altar comes in here ... and take off your shoes!"

Ahaz quickly snuffed his small light into the box of ashes. "I ... I couldn't see. In the darkness I grabbed a taper. Outside it's black." He kicked off his sandals.

Nicodemus strode toward him. "What do you mean, darkness? It's the middle of the day."

Ahaz dropped to his knees., "We have sinned. We are all doomed. God himself has taken away the sun!" He wailed and knelt until his forehead touched the floor.

"Ahaz, sit up. What are you babbling about? What has happened?"

"You knew. You tried to tell us. Now he is hanging on a cross." His body pulsed with deep sobs.

Nicodemus dropped before Ahaz. "I don't understand. Did they already put Jesus on trial?"

Ahaz thumped his chest. "We have killed the Messiah of God, and now God has sent darkness on the land. God sent a great prophet, but now he hangs on a Roman cross because of our plots. You tried to tell us. Please, Nicodemus, is there a sacrifice for me? Please forgive me!"

186

Nicodemus felt a cold chill. "Jesus has been crucified?" How could this have happened so quickly?

A great noise filled the chamber, the sound of a garment ripping—a harsh tearing sound. Nicodemus and Ahaz both stared at the curtain separating them from the Most Holy Place. It was parting from the top. The noise became louder as a the giant tear crept toward the floor. Ahab shrieked, "God forgive us!" The curtain parted, the final tear leaving a space the length of a man's arm between the pieces.

Ahaz wailed, "God has left us. The sacred place is open. God forgive! God forgive! We are doomed!"

Nicodemus trembled in fear. He stared at the gap in the curtain for a long time. This was the sacred barrier between man and the Holy place of God. He wondered what thing had caused God himself to tear open his very dwelling place.

Behind him Ahaz' moans turned to pitiful crying.

Nicodemus turned to the prostrate priest. "Ahaz, sit up." He pulled him to a sitting position. "We have witnessed something done by God. No human hand did this. This rend in the veil must be reported to the high priest. Go now and report what happened here." He rose and pulled Ahaz to his feet. "You have asked God's forgiveness and mine. You must settle with God, but I will forgive you—with difficulty, but I will forgive. Now go!"

Ahaz blubbered, "I will tell Caiaphas. How, I do not know." He grabbed Nicodemus' arm. "Thank you for forgiveness, I don't deserve it. I will remember this always."

Nicodemus placed his hand on the fat priest. "I do forgive you, my friend. I now know the one that has been crucified was the Son of God." He realized it was the first time he had openly confessed his belief in Jesus. He spoke softly. "He was God's Messiah." As he spoke, a jolt rushed through his whole body like a flood of white light. He had allowed his faith to take hold. A heavy burden lifted from his heart.

Ahaz straightened. "Then you have believed in him. Help my unbelief. I didn't know until ... until the cross ... and the darkness." He wiped his face with his sleeve. "You have called me friend. I was no friend. I voted for your removal. I ..."

"Those things are forgotten. Now go to the priests. Tell them what has happened. Soon it will be the Sabbath. They will plan to enter the great doors to the Holy Place. They must decide what to do."

Ahaz rushed to the door; turned once again to view the torn curtain, then bolted out.

* * *

Nicodemus remained in prayer for a long time, until the door behind him creaked opened.

His cousin, Joseph, walked quietly to him. "Nicodemus, I need your help. Jesus has been killed—I will explain more as we go—but, I have been given permission for us to take the body down from the cross and bury it."

Nicodemus rose. "Is it still dark outside?"

"There is darkness of soul in the city, but the light of the sun has returned. Come, Pilate had the thieves' legs broken, but Jesus had already died."

"He's dead? Are you certain?"

"A soldier made sure. He plunged a spear deep into his side. Yes, the hope of Israel is dead. Caiaphas and his friends requested the three bodies be removed before the Sabbath. Come. We have work to complete before sunset."

Nicodemus put his arm around Joseph's shoulder. "The spices my family kept so many years are for Jesus. They are in my home. We will use them to prepare his body for burial."

They both looked once more at the torn curtain, then left the sanctuary arm in arm.

*   *   *

The sun neared the horizon, ushering in the Sabbath. Four soldiers dragged the two bodies to a pit near the hill. The centurion stood beside the little band of women as they washed the body of the one called the Nazarene. There would be no mass grave for Jesus.

Joanna put her arm about Mary, the mother of Jesus. "We will take care of the preparation; you don't have to watch."

Mary drew a deep breath. "I must. He is the one God sent to me so very long ago." She gently pulled the crown of thorns from his head and pressed her forehead to his face.

Mary Magdalene tenderly wiped the blood from his wrists and side. Her tears fell on his chest.

The centurion spoke softly. "Should my men carry the body some place for you?"

Joanna shook her head. "Thank you. The two men coming up the hill will help us take the body when we finish washing it." She watched Nicodemus and Joseph climb the little hill, and recognized the burden they carried. As they approached, she said, "It is appropriate, my brother, that you bring the gift the wise men gave us. I never even considered this spice would be used in this way—but it is fitting."

*   *   *

It was cold inside the cave. Outside, darkness had descended when Nicodemus and Joseph poured the last of the frankincense and myrrh mixture into the folds of cloth covering Jesus' stiffening body. Joanna and Mary of Magdalene were wrapping the legs and the other two women, numb with grief, held the two torches.

Nicodemus placed the head covering over his Lord's serene face. "My cousin, when you bought this new tomb here near Jerusalem, I thought it a foolish thing. Now, I understand it was the will of God leading you to be the one to provide a final resting place for the one we hoped would be ..." Words choked in his throat.

The six of them faced the body. It lay on the stone shelf. The wind had risen and the trees were rustling, but none moved toward the cave's doorway.

The sound of heavy boots caused both men to move to the entrance. Four Roman soldiers stood outside.

"What are you men doing here?" Joseph demanded in the language of the Romans.

"We have been sent by the governor to set a seal on the tomb and guard it through the night. At second watch, we will be relieved."

"Who ordered this?"

The oldest of the four answered, "The request was made by the Jewish Council, to prevent his disciples from carrying his body away. They fear if the body is taken, some will claim he is resurrected."

"Resurrected?"

The words of Jesus flashed through Nicodemus mind. A seed must fall in the earth and die, and then it shall spring to life. But Jesus wasn't a seed—or was he?

The solder in charge spoke softly. "The governor has assured the Council he will make it secure." He examined the large circular stone at the mouth of the rock and then turned to Joseph. "Are you ready for us to set the seal on this tomb? Pilate has ordered us to make it as sure as we can. Please step outside."

Joseph's fist clenched. He dropped his head and led the others out through the low opening.

Mary Magdalene broke into sobs. Joanna held her close. Jesus' mother trudged up the hill headed back toward the city. The other women followed her. The three soldiers rolled the stone down the trench until it thumped into place. The other soldier mixed mortar to prevent the stone's removal.

The chill of the fall evening was intensified by the heaviness on Nicodemus' soul. He had finally accepted that this was truly God's son—the Messiah—now a corpse lying on the cold stone.

Chapter Twenty-Three

Sabbath

Nicodemus scrubbed his hands for the fourth time and let out a deep sigh. Would he ever forget this night? It was almost midnight before he crawled into bed. Deborah's warm body snuggled against him.

She jolted upright. "You're freezing!" She pulled back, sat up and stroked his cheek. "Tell me what's happened."

Nicodemus had trouble forming words. "What have we done? We are expected to be the people of God, the nation to receive God's Messiah ... and we have tortured him to death on a cross."

Deborah wiped the tears from his cheek with her sleeve. "My husband, I too, do not understand. I do remember him saying, 'A grain of seed has to fall into the ground and die to produce fruit.' It seems he faced death not as one defeated, but as one triumphant."

Nicodemus pondered her words. He dropped into a restless sleep with Deborah's fingers stroking his neck.

Nicodemus slept fitfully, locked in a dream he had not suffered through since childhood. A large snake was writhing on a pole. Before it a crowd of people were begging for mercy. Moses, the Lawgiver, raised his arms to heaven. Slowly, the figure of the snake changed into the body of the Nazarene. Then the words Nicodemus had heard from Jesus' own lips echoed across the barren rocks. "And I, if I be lifted up will draw all men unto myself." Someone in the crowd yelled, "Let his blood be on us and our children."

Deborah shook him awake. "You're dreaming Nicodemus. Wake up."

Nicodemus bolted upright. His body was drenched with sweat, yet he was shivering.

As best he could, Nicodemus recounted the dream. The trembling had subsided, the vision had not. "What have we done?" He slid from the bed. "I will not sleep more, I dare not."

Deborah slipped into her heavy robe. "Dawn will come soon." She added wood to the embers and blew them to life. Within minutes, she handed a hot drink to her husband and sat before him. "You told me, when you went to Jesus by night, he said that God didn't send him to the world to condemn it. Didn't that mean you too?"

"I was not a part of the Council that plotted to bring Jesus to the cross, but I did nothing to stop them. Don't you understand? I should have done something!"

It was the longest Sabbath day Nicodemus could remember. He did not attend the synagogue, being ceremonially unclean from handling the dead body. He still smelled the odor of death on him, though he had changed his garments and washed his hands over and over. He prayed, then pored over the scroll of Isaiah, the prophet that had spoken of the one Nicodemus now knew was the Christ.

Past midday Deborah brought him bread and fruit, but he refused to eat. She sat, legs crossed, before him. "My father says Isaiah spoke of the Messiah as a suffering one. Perhaps Jesus may have fulfilled a task in a way we didn't expect—when he was led like a lamb to be slaughtered."

A shudder went through Nicodemus. He'd pondered those words many times, but never with that meaning. He took her hands and kissed them. He shook his head; this woman understood things he did not.

*   *   *

With the setting sun, the lonely Sabbath ended. A soft knock announced Joseph's arrival. He slumped into the room.

Deborah kissed his cheeks in greeting. "Cousin, you look as though this has been a long day for you also. Come, I will tell Nicodemus you're here. May I bring you food? My husband hasn't eaten all day."

Joseph shook his head. "We will fast. It seems fitting."

Nicodemus sat dumb before his cousin.

Joseph broke the silence. "Most of the apostles have taken shelter at my home. They are shaken. Peter seems the most disturbed. I had never seen him weep before. As I came here, it seemed the whole city is in mourning. Some have spoken of seeing dead saints walking the streets. It is as though they're waiting for something, something they can't comprehend. Judas Iscariot's body is hanging beside the northern wall where he took his life."

"He's dead?" Deborah exclaimed.

"Ahaz, our old Council adversary, came to our home. He told me a curious story. He said that Caiaphas and Annas had paid Judas to betray the location of Jesus for thirty pieces of silver."

Nicodemus leaned forward. "Ahaz ... he was in on the plot?"

"I don't think he was in favor of it, but he witnessed it. Ahaz has changed. He told me he is convinced that Jesus was sent from God."

Nicodemus replied, "When I witnessed the temple veil being split, Ahaz was there with me. True, he's changed."

"Yes, and he said that after Pilate had ordered the crucifixion, Judas tried to return the silver to Caiaphas, but he refused to take the blood money. Judas threw it on the treasury floor."

Deborah muttered, "The price of betrayal was only the cost of a slave?"

The men were silent.

She shook her head, her voice rising. "The price of God's son was the price of a slave?"

*　*　*

It was early on the first day of the week when four women—Mary Magdalene, Mary the mother of James, Joanna and Salome—walked in the dim light from the northern gate of the city. They had just passed the gates when the ground under their feet shook violently.

Joanna tightened her grip on Mary Magdalene. "The whole earth is trembling at his death. Again God is showing his fury."

As they neared the grove descending to the rocky cliff, Salome asked, "How will we remove the stone? It's too heavy for us, and that seal cannot be easily broken."

The slope wound downward through the trees. When she reached the bottom, Mary Magdalene cried out, "The stone! Look! It's rolled away!"

All four stood gaped in amazement.

Mary Magdalene stole toward the opening.

Joanna looked around. "The soldiers guarding the tomb are gone."

Salome, clutching the spices she carried, followed Mary Magdalene to the tomb. She halted as Mary stood frozen in the opening. A bright glow lit the entrance. From within, a deep resonant voice asked, "Why do you seek the living among the dead?"

The women dropped to their knees. The voice spoke again. "Come, see the place where he lay." Joanna and Mary joined the others and peered into the tomb. Again the voice spoke. "Go, tell the others he is risen."

The napkin Joanna had placed over Jesus' face was neatly folded at one side. A thrill swept through her body—could it be, could he be alive?

Mary Magdalene turned, her eyes bright. Risen!—she repeated it over and over, then called, "You three go and find the others! I know where Peter and John are staying. I'll tell them." She glanced back at the light, then ran up the slight hill toward the city.

Mary Magdalene burst into the door where a group of disciples were praying. She cried, "They have taken the Lord out of the tomb and we don't know where they have put him."

Peter jumped to his feet. His forehead furrowed. "What are you saying? How could—?

John was already throwing on his cloak. "You have been to the tomb this early?"

Mary nodded vigorously and gave her account of the opened tomb and the angelic voice. Peter was the first out the door. John followed him, Mary close behind. All three rushed down the street. John passed him before they had reached the northern gate.

John stood panting before the open tomb, but Peter bolted by him. Jesus' burial wrappings were on the stone shelf. With amazement, they stared at each other.

Mary stood outside the tomb weeping as the two apostles walked back up the hill.

John spoke slowly. "He spoke of resurrection, but I thought ..."

Peter sighed. "We must find where they have taken him. Come, we must tell the others."

Tears filled Mary Magdalene's eyes as she trudged up the incline. Glancing ahead, she saw the feet of a man. It must be the gardener. She sobbed. "Sir, where have you taken him?"

A strangely familiar voice spoke her name. "Mary."

Recognition hit her like a wall. Her mouth dropped open and she looked up. "My Lord.! My Jesus!"

Jesus held his palms before him. "Touch me not, for I have not yet ascended to the Father. Go and tell the disciples I have risen."

Suddenly he was gone.

Mary stumbled forward. Her walk became a run, then a sprint.

Ten apostles were in the room with the disciples when Mary burst through the door. She felt the hot tears, but joy coursed through her body like a torrent. She exclaimed, "He is risen, I've seen him! He's alive! Jesus is risen!"

Chapter Twenty-Four

The Risen One

Joanna banged the door open and grabbed Deborah in her arms. "He's alive! Jesus is alive! The tomb is empty!"

Nicodemus turned to his sister in disbelief. "What—how? How can this be? He was dead." He felt like shouting. "I know. I handled his dead body." He took her by the shoulders. "Joanna, don't play with me."

Joanna, her face radiant, hugged both her brother and Deborah. "He's alive!" She almost danced as she embraced them. "Mary Magdalene actually saw him. Jesus is risen!" Her voice calmed, her finger raised. "I understand now. He spoke of his coming death, and we thought it was just another strange teaching. He really did die. But now, he is risen!"

Nicodemus slid to the low bench, covering his mouth. He whispered, "The Messiah has fulfilled the prophecy of the slain lamb." A thrill surged up his spine. "I'm beginning to understand. Yes, it makes sense."

* * *

Across the city, crowded into an upper room, the apostles, minus Thomas, sat in disbelief. Mary Magdalene, for the third time, explained what she saw. "I tell you the tomb was empty. I can't explain it any better than John did."

Peter clenched his fists. "The tomb was empty, but perhaps his ghost—" The feeling of fear and wonder filled those in the room.

Mary Magdalene shouted, "I saw him. He was standing there, and he was not a ghost!"

There was a knock on the chamber door. Everyone froze.

Peter grabbed his sword and moved toward the door. John, being closer, whispered,"Who's there?"

An excited voice answered, "We have seen Jesus. We talked to him."

John opened the door and two disciples pushed in. They were sweating and breathing hard. All those in the room relaxed as the two familiar men entered. One man plopped onto a cushion, panting. "We were on the road to Emmaus. There was a man—we didn't recognize him—he just joined us. As we went, he talked to us."

The other disciple interrupted. "I don't know why we didn't recognize who he was. He walked all the way to our town and opened our eyes to the scriptures. He told us the Messiah had to die and be raised."

The first man continued the story. "When we reached Emmaus, we invited him to stay the night with us. As we started to eat, we asked him to bless the food."

The second man interrupted again. "It was when he lifted his hands to bless the bread that we recognized who it was. It was Jesus."

The first disciple lifted his arms, his eyes wide. "When we realized who it was, he just ... disappeared."

The other interrupted. "—Into thin air, he just vanished. We left and came back here as fast as we could. Jesus is alive!"

The disciples looked stunned. Mary, her face radiant, raised her hands toward heaven. "Jesus lives. My Redeemer lives."

There was a slight movement behind John.

Inside the room—not near the door—Jesus stood smiling at the startled disciples. Lifting his hands he spoke gently. "Peace be with you."

Peter dropped to his knees. One by one, others knelt.

The women lifted their palms to Jesus. Mary sobbed for joy, tears trickling down her cheeks. "My Lord and my God!"

Jesus turned to the apostles. "As the Father has sent me, so I am sending you." He raised his hands and lifted his eyes upward. "Receive the Holy Spirit." His breath blew softly over them. A calm descended on the disciples as Jesus taught them late into the night. Then as quickly as he appeared, he vanished from their sight.

* * *

The news of the empty tomb had reached Caiaphas and his inner circle in another way. Four very frightened Roman soldiers stood before him.

"And you don't know how they opened the tomb, or where his body was taken?" the high priest raged.

One soldier shook his head. "There was an earthquake, and the next thing we knew, the stone was pulled back. When we looked into the tomb, no one was there."

Another cried, "We didn't go to sleep. We were wide awake, then ..." His voice trailed off.

Annas crossed the room, rubbing his hands. "Now the disciples will say he's alive." He pointed an accusing finger at the guards. "Are you sure you didn't see anyone else?"

They shook their heads.

He paced and then he wheeled around. "You didn't tell anyone else about this?"

The older soldier pleaded, "If Pilate hears of our failure, we'll be killed. He will not spare us for an instant."

Caiaphas bit his nails. After a silence, he pointed to the men. "You men are to tell anyone who asks you what happened that you fell asleep. While you slept his disciples came, opened the tomb, and carried the body away. Clear? We will give each of you fifty-pieces of silver provided you do exactly what we tell you."

"But for falling asleep on duty—"

Caiaphas raised his fist. "We'll take care of that. Just do as we say. But if any of you say anything more ..." His finger slid across his throat, the meaning was clear.

The soldiers slunk out. The group of Sadducees looked at one another. Annas ordered a servant, "Bring Ahaz in."

Ahaz looked around the room at the Sadducees. He dropped to a chair. "God will send a plague on all of us. We have killed the Messiah. We have plotted and God responded with blackness and earthquake, and now the temple veil is rent from top to bottom!"

The others looked stunned. Annas' eyes narrowed. "This is the report you brought us Friday evening." He looked around the room. "The veil is torn, both Caiaphas and I have seen it. How, we do not know. We suspect that somehow one of the apostles entered—"

Ahaz jumped to his feet. "I was in the Holy Place! I saw it tear from the top. It just split! No one touched it!" He thudded to his chair.

Caiaphas stood. "Did anyone else see this happen? Perhaps, you're mistaken."

Ahaz shook his head. "Nicodemus was there too. We watched it. I had been to the crucifixion at Golgotha and with the darkness I fled to the temple to pray. When I entered, the earth was still shaking. Then the veil started to tear. Fifty years ago, when we first dedicated the holy temple, I saw them hang that veil. God has deserted us." He sobbed openly.

Annas moved to his old friend. "My dear Ahaz, you must go home and rest. We have much to discuss. Go home and get some sleep." He helped Ahaz to his feet and ushered him to the door. When he returned he faced the others. "I am afraid Ahaz will no longer be of any use to us." He stroked his beard. "We must frighten these disciples of the Nazarene before general knowledge of the events of the last few days spreads."

Caiaphas took his seat. "If Nicodemus witnessed this tearing of the sacred veil, we must also silence him. Anyone have any suggestions?"

Annas said, "When Nicodemus stormed out of our last meeting of the assembly I thought he was leaving the Council permanently. Do you others agree?"

Several expressed agreement and Caiaphas stated, "Let's concentrate on those Galileans who were his apostles. I think we can intimidate them into silence. Does anyone know where they are?"

Annas said, "I'll send a message to our informers. Each of you, be especially aware of those who seem to follow Nicodemus' persuasions." He stroked his beard. "Some of the members of the Council are still uncomfortable with our actions of last week. We should keep our concerns within our inner circle. The full Sanhedrin will not meet again for five more weeks. By this time, we should have silenced this messiah talk."

* * *

Mary Magdalene and Salome prepared the meal for the large gathering in the chamber above. Joanna cut the bread. "The news of the resurrection is all over the city. Even in the market, everyone is talking about it. His resurrection is the gossip of the marketplace."

Mary arranged the dates on a platter. "I hear the body of Judas Iscariot is hanging near the northern gate. No one has gone to remove it. It has been rotting there for five days now."

Joanna shook her head. "With this hot wind, someone needs to remove it before the stench reaches the city." She sliced more bread. "Even the children know this is the one who betrayed Jesus. Did you hear, the priests took the thirty pieces of silver and bought the Potter's Field where he hangs? It is to be a place to bury the poor."

Mary lifted her tray. "With all the apostles staying here, it will be hard to hide their location much longer. They are getting restless." Joanna knew this was true but they needed one another—she certainly did.

The two women entered the upper room. They saw that Thomas was with the other apostles. A heated discussion was in process.

Thomas clenched his teeth. "Unless I see him, I'm just not going to believe he is alive. Unless I place my fingers in the nail prints, I won't believe." He froze mid-sentence, his mouth wide.

Standing beside the wall was Jesus. "Peace be to you, Thomas."

Thomas, went pale and gasped. "Jesus!"

Jesus beckoned to Thomas. "Come, give me your hand. Place your fingers in the holes where the nails were, and put your hand in my side."

Thomas choked. "My Lord and my God!"

Jesus took Thomas' hand and placed his finger in the wounds. Then with Thomas' face in his hands, he looked deep into his eyes. "Blessed are those who have not seen, and yet believe." For once, Thomas was speechless.

Jesus sat with the eleven and taught them. Late that evening, he rose and lifted his hands. "I will meet you in Galilee." While they watched, he vanished before them.

Chapter Twenty-Five

Fishermen

Jesus did many other miraculous signs in the presence of his disciples, which are not recorded in this book. But these are written that you might believe that Jesus is the Christ, the Son of God, and that by believing you might have life in his name.
John 20:30, 31

* * *

John stood on the beach watching the blue waters of the lake turn dark as the sun dropped toward the western hills. He turned to James. "It's been three weeks since he rose from the dead. We came to Galilee, where is Jesus?"

James shrugged. "No idea. The women who came from Jerusalem say people all over Judea have seen him." The two walked to the other five apostles standing by the boat. Peter wandered to the shore.

Nathaniel shook his head and whispered, "Look at Peter. I've never seen him act so ... so frustrated. He lacks purpose."

Peter threw a rock across the water and turned to the others. "I just don't like sitting idly and waiting. How long will it before we know what we're supposed to be doing?" He slung another stone so that it skipped across the water.

Thomas shook his head. "I don't know either, but I'll tell you this. I'll never, never doubt him again. He said to meet him here in Galilee, so I'll wait."

Peter joined the others and pulled his belt tight. "I'm going fishing. Anyone joining me?" He plodded to his father's boat which was rocking in the gentle waves. Nathaniel rose, followed by Thomas, James and John. Finally, seven men pushed the small boat into the lake. Peter took the main oar, while the sons of Zebedee raised the small single sail.

Lowering the nets, they drifted toward the north, as the sun sank behind the hills. James and John kept the net from tangling, making the final cast of the evening. The sky darkened.

Thomas, lying back against the prow, gazed at the appearing stars. "Surely he wanted us to carry his message, but what do we say? Where do we start?"

John's fingers trailed in the water. In their three years together, there was so much to remember. He watched Peter adjust the small oil lamp and tie it to the mast. "Peter, do you remember what he promised us the last time he was with us?"

Peter turned. John watched his puzzled expression. "What do you mean?"

John sat upright. "He told us we would be able to recall all that he did and said."

"Sure, I remember."

"I was just thinking about it. I can call to mind the entire time since he selected us, almost everything." James moved a coil of rope. "Yesterday, I found I was able to recite the entire lesson he taught on the mountain. Do you remember the time when the three of us were with him and Moses and Elijah appeared? It's as clear as though it were yesterday."

Nathaniel pulled his tunic tight. "You told us a little about that, and I wondered why just the three of you went up the mountain and not all of us. At the time, we were so busy teaching people, I didn't think much about it."

Thomas added, "Do you recall, when none of us could heal that boy who was thrashing around in the dirt, and Jesus and you three came back? He said we weren't able to because we didn't pray enough."

The waves gently rocked the boat. Each dropped into his own memories. Finally Nathaniel broke the stillness. "When that boy shrieked as he went into seizures and then lay still, I thought he'd died."

Peter said, "That's what we all thought. But when Jesus lifted him and he stood before us. I will always see the joy of his father as he hugged him in his arms I'll never forget that as long as I live."

Everyone again lapsed into silence.

Several times throughout the night they checked the nets, but finally just drifted in the moonlight. By moonset all had dropped off to sleep, nets still empty.

False dawn was breaking when Peter, clothed only in his undergarment pulled in the nets. "Not a single fish, just empty nets. I hate waiting for something to happen."

On the shore, a dim fire flickered to life. In the glow they saw the figure of someone working over the flames. The figure straightened and called, "Friends, have you any fish?"

John squinted at the shore, several bowshots away. "Not a one," he yelled.

The man called, "Throw your nets on the right side and you'll find some."

Peter, who had the net in his hands, sighed. He paused, grumbled, then shrugged and flung the net to the right side of the boat. He turned to awaken the other apostles, but before he could, the slack rope in his hands jerked and almost pulled him off his feet. John saw the look on Peter's face. His mouth gaped open. Peter threw his weight against the rope. He braced his feet and began tugging and yelled, "You men help!"

James, John and Andrew jumped to their feet and grabbed the lee rope and pulled. John froze and stared at the net. "It's full! Look at those fish!" He dropped the rope, turned and stared wide-eyed at the man on the shore. "It's the Lord!"

By now, the thrashing fish were breaking the surface and all the other men were hauling at the ropes.

Peter turned to the shore and stared at the tall figure on the beach. He grabbed his outer cloak, threw it about him and plunged into the water. John watched his strong stroke pulling him toward the beach. James and Andrew clung to the net as the others rowed frantically toward shore. Thomas had begun throwing fish aboard, and James yelled, "Stop, you're going to sink us, we're only a little ways out. Get another oar and row." In the confusion, the heavy boat made slow headway toward land.

Andrew cautioned, "Careful, that net's going to break. Look at the size of those fish!" As the boat reached the shallows, Peter waded out and grabbed the bulging net and dragged the surging mass to shore.

Jesus laughed as he watched the apostles wrestle the net into the shallows. Several others joined Peter and together they got the net full of fish to the shore. Peter dropped the rope and rushed to Jesus. He fell at his feet. "My Lord." His face almost touched the ground.

Jesus bent down and pulled him to his feet.

Jesus cooked several fish as the disciples warmed around the fire. "Bring some of the fish you have just caught." Peter went to retrieve a few and Jesus beckoned; "All of you, come, have breakfast."

Jesus' buoyant mood enlivened the conversation as they ate. Later, they watched a pile of fish bones blacken in the coals.

John leaned back against the boat, remembering the first great catch when Jesus had commanded them to leave the boat, the nets, and their fathers, to follow him. He fondly recalled the words that had changed their lives: "Come and follow me and I will make you fishers of men." That was three long, eventful years ago.

As the sun warmed the beach, Jesus stood. The apostles sat in a circle around him. He turned to Peter. "Simon, son of Jonas, do you truly love me more than these?" His hand pointed to the fish.

Peter's face flushed and John sensed his embarrassment.

Peter's mouth dropped open and he stammered, "Lord, you know I love you."

Jesus' eyes bored in. "Feed my lambs."

Then Jesus placed his hand on Peter. "Simon, son of Jonas, do you truly love me?"

Peter's brow furrowed. "Yes, you know I love you."

Jesus replied, "Take care of my sheep."

The third time Jesus asked, "Simon, son of Jonas, do you love me?"

All of the apostles watched Peter as color rose in his cheeks. Peter just stared at the teacher. His troubled voice pleaded, "Lord, you know I love you!"

The voice came gently, "Feed my sheep." He took Peter by the shoulders and moved his face close. "I tell you the truth, when you were young you dressed yourself and went where you wanted, but when you are old, you will stretch out your hands and someone else will dress you and lead you where you do not want to go." He looked around the men. "Follow me."

In the next hour, John listened as Jesus reignited passions he had felt at that first calling. Jesus stood silently studying each face in turn. Then he raised his hands. "Go again to Jerusalem."

Warmth surged through John at being near his master again. But arrest and possibly death awaited them in Jerusalem. He looked at the other faces and a thrill raced through him. The others were eager —they were ready for what was ahead.

Chapter Twenty-Six

Ascension

The eleven apostles and the small band of faithful women neared Jerusalem. Joanna sensed the excitement she always experienced when she saw the holy city, the great white temple rising above the walls. The morning sun reflected from the golden eastern face. Ahead, the Jaffa Gate thronged with people from all over the Jewish world. Pentecost was but eleven days away, and this was the time of the ingathering of Jews from all nations. People from far away— turbaned Parthian, dark-skinned Ethiopians, and Arabs in flowing robes—crowded the road. She could smell the various peoples, and wondered what made their aromas so different.

Before, it had always been Jesus in the lead, but now a bold Peter strode ahead. Joanna turned to Mary Magdalene. "Please stay with my family in the city. Nicodemus will welcome you. He is still walking through his own journey to faith, but his heart is with us." She felt the warmth of the sun, but a deeper inner flush warmed her even more as she imagined seeing the risen Lord once again. "He said he would go before us to Jerusalem. Do you suppose he will appear at the temple?"

Mary spoke, an irenic look on her face. "I don't know, but what I do know is, he will be with us once again. That's enough for me." She gave Joanna's hand a squeeze. "I will be pleased to stay with your family. I like your brother, and I look forward to meeting your whole family."

Ahead, Nathaniel, always the first in song, started singing one of the songs of ascent from the Psalms of David:

If the Lord had not been on our side when men attacked us,

When the anger flared against us, they would have swallowed us alive;

The flood would have engulfed us, the torrent would have swept over us,

The raging waters would have swept us away.

By the time he reached the second phrase, most of the apostles had joined in the song. Even some of the sojourners walking along lifted their voices, many in varying melodies, but all with the same words. Their sound rose in joyous praise.

To Joanna's left, a tall man, his face darkened by the desert sun, sang with a strange accent. On the other side a huge black man with booming voice joined with his own melody. All the voices wove an enchanting harmony. She almost laughed at the different ways some words were spoken. Somehow it was comforting to hear people—many total strangers—join in the Psalm, no matter how different their races.

Reaching the gates, Peter walked to a slight rise. The others gathered around him. "Some of us will go to Bethany. Others will be staying in the city. Remember, the Jews are still searching for us, so be careful. Tomorrow, around noon, we'll meet on the Mount of Olives. Jesus has given instructions, he will meet us there." He gestured to Joanna. "Will you women bring bread and wine?"

She beamed and nodded. Joanna felt a thrill. She would again be serving the master. Her own eagerness was reflected in the faces of the other women. The Lord would again be with them. They would break bread together.

* * *

In the usually sedate Sanhedrin chamber there was confusion. Caiaphas stood thudding his staff on the marble floor. "This session will come to order. Sit down. Be silent."

Nicodemus didn't want to sit or be quiet, but finally took his place.

Across the hall, Gamaliel had been waiting. He rose.

The murmuring ceased.

He paused for a moment until the chamber was silent.

Gamaliel's eyes swept the assembly. "Fellow members of this body, selected by the Jewish people to bring order and justice to this nation, we have been negligent in our duty."

Several of the Council grumbled.

"We have let our leaders plot, then sentence to death an innocent man." His voice rose. "Even the Romans deemed him guiltless. To cover this crime we have allowed our own members to be defamed." His eyes were moist as he turned to Nicodemus.

Nicodemus fairly glowed. Gamaliel had finally come to his defense. He'd felt so deserted when his own father-in-law had remained silent during his time of ostracism.

Gamaliel spoke softly. "I yield to one who can now testify." He turned to his son-in-law, motioning for him to stand. He raised his palm to his son-in-law and took his seat.

Nicodemus rose. He spread his hands to his fellow members. "I have always felt the honor of being a part of this great court. We have been ones selected to find the truth and proclaim it. In the matter of the crucifixion of the Nazarene, I believe we have killed one sent by God."

Another murmur swept the chamber, but Nicodemus raised his palm. "Concerning the charge that somehow the apostles of Jesus ripped the holy veil in the temple, both Ahaz and I were present when it happened. No one else was in the Holy Place, and we watched the holy curtain tear from top to bottom. No hand touched it." He looked around the room. "Except perhaps ... the hand of God."

Ahaz struggled to his feet. "This is exactly what we saw. At the time of the midday, the time of darkness over our city and the earthquake, I entered the temple. Nicodemus and I watched the dividing of the great curtain." He looked around; then dropped back to his seat.

Joseph rose and stood beside his cousin. "And I was present as interpreter for the trial of the Nazarene. Pontius Pilate himself said he found no cause for death in him. It was at your insistence"—his finger pointed like an arrow to the High Priests—"this innocent Nazarene was crucified."

It took a long time for the chamber to quiet. Finally, Annas stood, his voice subdued. "We will call an assembly to investigate the matters of the last month. For now, we still bear the responsibility to guard our nation's future. Some have reported sightings of one who poses to be the risen Nazarene, and today the Galileans who followed him have been seen in the city. We will need to watch them closely. Remember, Rome will not tolerate insurrection. Their armies would welcome the excuse to march in and slaughter our people. In ten days, Pentecost will be here, and the Roman armies are watching this Council."

* * *

The next morning was a beautiful clear day, with only a few scattered clouds. From the Mount of Olives, the city of Jerusalem spread before the followers. The women had carried bread for fifty. Joanna was glad they had brought enough—the crowd was large. The followers were seated or standing on the crest of the hill surrounding the apostles. The women moved among them to serve.

Peter rose and extended his arms. "Followers of Jesus, we are here as instructed by our Lord. He has commanded us to wait on this mount. Let us pray and thank God for this day and this food."

Instead of closing her eyes, Joanna's eyes studied the sky. She recalled that Jesus had often prayed in this manner.

When Peter finishing his brief prayer, Joanna lowered her eyes. Standing before Peter was Jesus.

Joanna moved quickly to offer the master a piece of bread and he smiled as his hand touched hers. She laughed as a flush of joy coursed through her.

He lifted the bread to heaven and, in his own unique way, pronounced the blessing. He walked among the followers, taking time to gaze into each face.

Joanna wiped her face with her sleeve. She had not allowed tears for many years, but now she couldn't hold the torrent that flooded down her cheeks.

Jesus' hands reached out toward the apostles. He commanded, "Do not leave Jerusalem, but wait for the gift my Father has promised, which you have heard me speak about. For John baptized you with water. Soon you will be baptized with the Holy Spirit."

Jesus' robe touched Joanna as he walked by. Her hand automatically reached up. He took it and held it for a long moment.

He turned to face his apostles, his voice firm. "Go into all the world and tell others about me, baptizing them in the name of the Father, the Son and the Holy Spirit, and I will be with you to the end of the world." He lifted his arms higher and looked toward heaven.

Joanna blinked to clear her eyes. Something was happening. His body looked different—somehow taller. Then she realized; he was rising into the air. Now he was above the crowd. He was moving upward. Jesus was rising toward heaven. She and the others stood frozen, gazing upward, watching his figure grow smaller and smaller. A little cry escaped her lips as Jesus disappeared into a cloud.

The disciples were hushed, until a powerful voice broke the silence. Everyone turned.

Two men dressed in dazzling white stood behind them. "You men of Galilee; why do you look into heaven? This same Jesus who has been taken to heaven will come back in the same way you have seen him go."

*   *   *

Across the Kidron Valley, standing on the parapet of the temple, a small band of priests watched the crowd across on the Mount of Olives. Nicodemus and Joseph stood beside Ahaz. They saw the crowd stop on the crest and watched the women moving among them. While they observed, more priests joined the watchers.

Nicodemus pointed. "That's Peter, and some of the other apostles are with him. They're just standing. What are they waiting for?

Joseph cried, "Look, the one in the center! That's Jesus, He's back with them."

One of the other priests blurted, "That's the Nazarene. I'd recognize him anywhere."

Ahaz said, "I wish I could hear what he's saying!"

They watched in silence, then Joseph shouted, "Look! He ... he's rising. He's going up into the air!"

Nicodemus felt a chill. "He's ascending toward heaven." He put his arm around the quivering Ahaz. "He has risen from the dead. Now He returns to God."

Ahaz whispered, "He returns to Heaven."

Chapter Twenty-Seven

Pentecost

Jesus did many other things as well. If every one of them were written down, I suppose that even the whole world would not have enough room for the books that would be written.
   John 21:25

The market near Joseph's house was busy, as it usually was on the first day of the week. But this day, the Day of Pentecost, the street was teeming with people from all over the Mediterranean world. The languages were as diverse as the clothing. Nicodemus and Joseph pushed their way through the throng to the fruit stand and picked several apples. The woman behind the stack of fruit turned toward Nicodemus. For a brief moment he thought he recognized her.

He gave her two coppers. She shook her head and handed one back. "Only one."

Joseph took one of the apples and polished it on his sleeve as they moved up the street. "This fruit is delicious. It comes from the slopes of Mount Hermon. God is good. I love this time of year, our Feast of Ingathering." He bit into the apple and turned to his cousin. "Did you recognize the seller?"

Nicodemus' brow furrowed and he shook his head. "Somewhat."

"If she were wearing jewelry and eye darkening?"

"Cloe?"

"Her life is changed, like so many others." He took another bite. "Yesterday in our synagogue, the talk was all of Jesus and his ascension. Several had witnessed it. Two of our members were on the Mount of Olives when he rose into the sky. I haven't seen such excitement in that synagogue in years."

Nicodemus finished his apple. "It was also the talk of the congregation where Deborah and I attend. There were many stories—some exaggerated, some disbelieving—all disquieting. I understand that a number of apostles were seen teaching in the temple court last evening."

The two had almost reached the steps leading to the lower temple court when Deborah rushed up, her breath coming in gasps. "Nicodemus, I'm so glad I found you. I went with Joanna to a prayer meeting this morning. The strangest things have happened. " She paused to gain her breath, and both men moved with her to a small bench near the stairs.

"Please, my wife, speak slowly and tell us."

Deborah took a deep breath. "Almost a hundred of us were gathered in Joseph's large room. The apostles were discussing the replacement of Judas. One named Matthias was selected and Peter and John prayed over his appointment. We were all praying when this strange looking fire appeared."

Joseph stiffened. "A fire in my house?"

"No, not a fire. It just looked like fire. It was going up from the apostles' heads."

Nicodemus took her shoulder. "Fire from their heads? When was this?"

"It looked like fire, and it was just a short time ago. The apostles started talking but their speech was different."

Joseph frowned. "How different?"

"I don't know. You speak many languages, but I know it was not the languages that I speak. Anyway, all of the rest of us didn't know what to do. I rushed to find you. This is so strange, but so much happening ... I just don't understand."

Without warning, a sound like a roaring of a wind echoed through the street. Nicodemus turned toward the open street ahead near the wide steps leading to the temple. Others were looking toward the sound and pointing. Both Nicodemus and Joseph took Deborah's arm and pushed forward to investigate. The crowd was surging toward the noise.

Nicodemus felt an ominous tightening in his neck. The roar was like a desert wind storm, yet no wind blew. He stopped abruptly. Before him, standing on the steps were several of the apostles.

Peter lifted his hands and the roaring slowly died away. One by one, the apostles addressed the crowd, only they were not speaking any language that Nicodemus understood. Even Joseph looked confused.

Nicodemus muttered, "What language is he speaking?"

Joseph shook his head. "I've heard that language, but I don't know for sure." A fruit vendor nearby jokingly chided, "These men are filled with new wine." Many of the crowd turned and scowled at his attempt at humor.

A man pointed to James and whispered to his companion. "He's speaking the language of Cyrene. He looks like a Galilean. How does he know my language?"

A band of turbaned people near the wall who were listening to Thomas turned. "That man is speaking Syrian."

Joseph took Nicodemus' arm. "Over there, that's Nathaniel and he's speaking the language of the Greeks. I understand him, but how?"

Peter's voice rose. He turned toward the street vendor. "These men are not drunken, this is what was spoken by the prophet Joel 'In the last days I will pour out my Spirit on all people.'"

Nicodemus had puzzled over that passage many times. Then he realized that a crowd of several thousand were paying rapt attention to the apostle.

Peter finished the quotation and continued. "Men of Israel, listen to this: Jesus of Nazareth was a man accredited by God to you by miracles, wonders and signs which God did through Him, as you yourselves know."

Nicodemus looked around the crowd. Many not only understood the words, they were in agreement.

Peter raised his arms. "This man was handed over to you by God's set purpose and foreknowledge." His finger swept the crowd. "And you, with the help of wicked men, put him to death by nailing him to the cross."

A murmur went through the crowd. Nicodemus felt a hot blade rush up his own spine. His nation, the ones who should have understood, should have welcomed the Messiah. They had been the ones to kill him. The crowd was deathly still.

Peter's voice became calm. "But God raised him from the dead."

Nicodemus watched Ahaz and several other members of the Council standing just to the left. Ahaz' head bobbed in agreement.

Next Peter quoted from David and carefully explained the prophecy of the Christ. His voice echoed off the walls as he proclaimed, "Therefore, let all the house of Israel be assured of this: God has made this Jesus, whom you crucified, both Lord and Christ!"

Ahaz wailed, "My brothers, what shall we do?" The cry sounded all over the crowded street.

"We have killed the one we have waited for."

"Forgive us, Lord, our sin is great."

"Have compassion, oh God! Mercy!"

Peter raised his hands again and the crowd quieted. His voice was pleading. "Repent and be baptized, every one of you in the name of Jesus Christ, for the forgiveness of your sins. And you will receive the gift of the Holy Spirit. The promise is to you and your children and all who are visiting from afar—for all whom the Lord our God will call."

The apostles mixed with the crowd and began talking to them. John was near Ahaz when the priest demanded, "I believe, I believe! I beg you, baptize me now. The pool of Bethesda is near." He dropped to his knees. "I ask you now, please."

Nicodemus grabbed Joseph's shoulders and hugged him. "My cousin, we need to go with old Ahaz. I think I too need to be plunged into the water." He felt the hand of Deborah.

She said, "I too will be baptized." Joy filled her eyes. "I will join you. Come, I want your friend John to be the one to bury us under the water."

Nicodemus pressed toward John. He and Deborah joined Ahaz as they headed toward the pool of Bethesda. James led another group of excited people behind them. Within minutes, they reached the pool. Many stood along the edges. Beside the pool, Ahaz placed his hand on John's shoulder.

Ahaz pleaded, "Please, my friend, I need the cleansing of my wretched soul. More than all these. I am utterly guilty of crucifying God's messenger. Please baptize me first."

John smiled and led Ahaz into the pool. He turned to the chubby priest. "Will you now confess that you believe that Jesus is the God-sent savior of the world?"

Ahaz looked thoughtful, then proclaimed, "I believe with all my heart that Jesus is God's son."

John plunged the priest under the water. He came up, a wide grin on his face. He lifted his hands as he waded to the edge repeating, "Thank you! Thank God!"

John motioned to Nicodemus and Deborah. They waded into the pool together. Placing his hand on Nicodemus, John spoke so that all heard. "And do you, Nicodemus, believe that Jesus is God's Messiah?"

Nicodemus' voice bounced from the pillars. "I believe that Jesus is the Christ the Son of God!"

Deborah, in a clear voice added, "And I accept that Jesus is God's only Son, sent to save this world, and forgive me."

John baptized them both. Nicodemus put his arm around his wife and they waded to the side of the long pool. A large crowd stood in line waiting for their own immersion. At the opposite end of the pool, James was baptizing others.

Deborah, looking at her soaked husband, shook her head. "My husband, you have just thoroughly doused your best robe."

Nicodemus lifted his fist and replied, "That, my love, was exactly what I meant to do. My priestly robe now has a new meaning to me. It has been cleansed by God."

Partially hidden behind a column, watching the proceedings, Saul of Tarsus stroked his cheek. This heresy was gaining popularity more than the Council had realized. Caiaphas was correct; Ahaz would be of no use to their group now. He turned and hurried toward the temple.

Ahaz, standing in the pool, started to ascend the stairs. Just as he reached the landing he lost his balance. Flailing his arms in a wide arc, he fell backward with a huge splash. There was dead silence as he emerged spluttering. A grin spread across his face and he shouted, "Hallelujah!" The onlookers roared in laughter.

Ahaz yelled, "All of you are invited to my home for the Pentecost meal. All of you!"

Nicodemus called out, "His house is by the Hulda Gate, and my wife and I will help in the preparations." He hugged the fat priest. John and Joseph joined the embrace.

Joseph laughed. "If this isn't a scene; Jesus' apostle and three Pharisees, all brothers."

John pointed to the waiting crowd. "Joseph and Nicodemus, I will need your help. Almost a hundred are here to be immersed. Will you help me?"

Nicodemus smiled. "Why not? I have been the one who has been wrestling with doubt longer than any in this city." He faced John. "It will be my honor to assist you in this noble task."

He turned to Deborah who was drying her hair beside the pool. "I will assist John here. You go with Ahaz and help in the preparations for our feast. My cousin and I will join you later."

On that day, Pentecost 33 AD, over 3,000 were added to the church in the city of Jerusalem. In the next decade, the followers of this new Way were to spread over the entire Roman world.